The Smoke Road

Copyright D.F. Bissonnette 2017 ©

Danielle.Bissonnette@Gmail.com

All rights reserved. No part of this document may be reproduced or transmitted in any form or by any means, electronic, mechanical, photocopying, recording, or otherwise, without prior written permission of Danielle Bissonnette.

This is a work of fiction; any similarity between characters in this book and living or recently deceased persons is purely coincidental.

The Smoke Road

For William Frederik Priestly, my Grandfather

1875

The locusts came at noon. Jabber watched the cloud, its twists, its turns, its undulations, and made a game of spotting forms and faces: a maddened bull, a caballero on a rearing horse, a skull, a dead man lying on a cart.

The wagons trundled on beneath the prairie sun, snaking west. The men and older children walked beside the wheels, kicking rocks from the ruts and the bleached bones of failed oxen left weather.

"Think it'll move on, Pa?" Jabber pointed to the cloud.

Jacob Walk watched the cloud. He watched it rise. He watched it fall. He watched it curl back and collapse on itself. "Go find your sister."

Jabber ran back nine wagons.

Bessie walked with Colleen O'Fallon. Her chestnut braid swung side to side like a rope beneath her blue bonnet. Colleen's hair hung wild--a mess of copper curls, bleached by the sun and dry as last year's cotton.

The dark cloud descended. The sound was like pecan husks falling on a dirt floor, thousands of them--millions and it swallowed all other sounds, the creaking buckboards, the hissing wheels in the packed earth. Writhing with beating wings it settled on the land like dust, eating all before it. Bessie screamed and beat her hair. They crawled in her chocolate braids, biting her fingers and ears. They clawed at her gingham dress, the brown juices from their jaws running down her arms with the blood, staining her dress; staining her. Jabber chased his sister, striking them with his hat, but more came to take their place. He beat them until the locusts ate his hat.

Colleen cried out as the locusts crawled across her face, biting the skin around her eyes. She struck the locusts, and when there were no more crawling in her hair, across her face, she struck herself. She clawed her skin until the blood ran and fistfuls of carrot-colored hair lay on the ground. Patrick O'Fallon stuffed her under the wagon.

The mule threw it's head and groaned, flicking its ears. The menfolk rushed to unhitch the stock. Corra Walk leapt from the wagon, her swollen belly bouncing beneath a gingham dress. She unhitched the oxen.

"Keep'm off the stock and out of the stores," Pa Walk yelled as he beat the locusts with his coat.

"It's the end times what like the padre said," Colleen O'Fallon cried and covered her eyes.

Bessie and Jabber crawled under their wagon with their mother.

The men tore the shirts from their backs and tied them around ax handles. They dipped them in kerosene and lit them, forming a circle wielding fire to beat back the swarm. The locusts fell like pine cones, their wings smoldering and crumpled. Their legs singed and crippled, some hopped with one leg, others crawled.

The women and children gathered them in their aprons and hats.

Jabber squished the heads.

That night they ate fried locust for supper with beans and hard biscuits.

Jabber laid on an old horse blanket as the women cleaned the pans and the tin plates. The men smoked and talked about black earth and golden wheat. Colleen O'Fallon sat on the back of the trap, with a stained shawl covering her head, quoting scripture as she rocked back and forth.

"Patrick O'Fallon never did anything so cruel as to bring that woman west," Bessie said, "They should have stayed in Boston."

Jabber looked at the old gray mule, it's ribs showing as it gnawed a bit of scrub. "Pa says the stockman cheated them in St. Lewis because they were Catholics."

Bessie watched the stars cross the sky then she looked over at Mr. O'Fallon. "That ain't why," Bessie said.

...

Dawn smelled of sage and smoke. It was dry and the weeds rattled like old chicken bones under the porch on those hot July afternoons, back home in Lexington. A blue haze hung in the south west above a thin band of white. Jabber shaded his eyes.

Pa hitched up the oxen and checked their hooves. The lead ox, the one called Bud, had a sore on his shoulder behind the hump. The flies crawled over it, tasting the yellow crust forming at the edges. Pa hopped up in the wagon and pulled out one of the flannel bedsheets. He cut a swatch out about the size of his hand. He slathered honey on it.

"Talk to him, keep his mind off the damned flies," Pa said.

Jabber pet Bud's foreleg and said. "Ain't that much further, Bud, then it's gonna be high grass and sweet water, all the way to the sea."

Bud flicked his ears and heaved out a warm breath. Pa laid that flannel on Bud's shoulder. Bud groaned and threw his head, and Pa hitched the yolk further up his neck.

"Can't we rest him, Pa?" Jabber asked.

Pa rubbed Bud's shoulder. "Bud's tough, and we got to get through the mountains before the snows come."

Jabber shaded his eyes again. "Those mountains?" He pointed north.

Pa shook his head. "Can't see them yet. They're over there, beyond the salt flats." He pointed to a hazy band of sky beyond-beyond in the great blue unknown of California.

The women cooked breakfast over a cow-chip fire. The burning paddies smelled sweet, like hay and prairie grasses. They cooked biscuits and ham-steaks. Colleen spoke scripture as she cooked. Mr. O'Fallon sat down on a rock some ways from his wife to eat his ham-steak and biscuit. He ate alone.

Mamma stretched her back after breakfast and placed a hand on her belly. "The baby's coming before California, that's sure as judgement day."

Pa nodded.

"What you going to call it?" Jabber asked.

"Seth. His name is going to be Seth," Pa said.

"I am not naming my baby after your father," Mamma said. "Don't you make that face at me, Jacob. From the day we married till the day they laid him in the ground, your father never had a kind word for me or any of my kin. That ain't speaking ill of the dead, it's the God's-honest-truth. "

"If that one's a boy," Pa said. "His name is Seth. If it ain't, then you name it whatever you want."

Mamma crossed her arms. "I hope it's girl. Hope they're all girls from this one to the last, and I hope your father--."

"Watch your mouth," Pa said.

Mamma narrowed her eyes. "Rests in the bosom of the Lord."

The wagons rolled at half-past-five and one star remained in the sky--a bright star, white and unwavering. The wagons followed its descent.

Jabber walked beside Bud and whispered in his ear about that tall grass and the sweet water waiting just beyond those mountains in California.

...

Heat wavered off the salt flats forming a lake that got no nearer.

"It's a mirage," Bessie said.

"You're not back with Mrs. O'Fow-on," Jabber said.

Bessie shook her head. "Mamma needs me more than Colleen does."

Jabber looked at their mother, holding her belly with her eyes closed and her brows furrowed as the wagon rattled over the ruts in the salt.

The sun beat overhead and the powder-fine salt dusted everything. It stung the eyes and the nose. The oxen and cattle groaned and snorted. Jabber scratched his wet parts and they burned.

Something gray stuck out of the white up ahead. Jabber squinted at it. "What's that, Bessie?"

Bessie shaded her eyes. "Can't tell."

"Is it another Meerwad?" Jabber asked.

"Meer-hodge, Jasper, Meer-hodge," Bessie said.

Jabber scrunched up his face.

Bessie fanned herself with her bonnet. "Maybe once we get to California, we can find you a doctor--help you talk right."

Jabber scratched his arms and the back of his neck.

"Stop picking at it, it's all red. What happened to your hat?" Bessie asked.

Jabber folded his hands and pouted. "The woe-custs ate it."

The salt dust scurried across the playa in snakes and beetles. Nothing grew in the salt. Nothing lived in the salt.

The gray blob rose like a steeple of clay. Pillows of gray and white salt crusted around something rectangular. Jabber made out a wheel half buried in the playa and an axle, then a withered foreleg.

Pa pulled up the wagon and looked at it.

Mamma righted herself, holding her belly with one hand and pushing herself up with the other.

"How long you think it's been here, Pa?" Jabber asked.

"Long time," Pa said. He flicked the slack reins. "Walk on."

The oxen groaned in their harnesses. The wheels rolled. Mamma closed her eyes and held her belly, muttering something about Lot's wife.

. . .

Night fell on a white world. Jabber walked across the salts, glowing like the surface of the moon. Bessie cooked dinner while Momma lay on a quilt in the trap. The men smoked and poured over the map by lantern light.

"We should travel by night," said Mr. O'Fallon, "We can take turns sleeping and be across the damn thing before noon tomorrow."

Colleen O'Fallon sat in her wagon muttering to the night beyond moon and stars, worrying her black beads. Her prayers carried only a little ways beyond her lips.

Bessie handed Jabber a tin plate with some beans and salt beef. Bessie took a plate to Colleen. Colleen rocked back and forth under that blanket, talking-- sometimes to Bessie, sometimes as if Bessie wasn't there. Bessie sighed and brought the plate back.

"That was a good thing you did," Mamma said after the men set to their supper.

"You think Mr. O'Fallon would like to join us?" Bessie asked.

Mamma looked at her and then at Mr. O'Fallon as he struggled to make a fire. "Why don't you go ask him."

Bessie nodded.

"Don't encourage it," Pa said.

"I ain't encouraging nothing. It's Christian charity."

"No it ain't. You know it ain't. Tomorrow Bessie walks with us."

Mamma glowered at Pa. She looked down at Jabber. "Go on then, you bring him that plate."

The men talked after dinner. They smoked and consulted. Bessie gathered white salt crystals from the ground and placed them in a mason jar.

The wagon train traveled under the full moon across a ghost desert. The salt lay like snow over everything and as they walked, blue fire skittered over the ears of the stock and flashed among their coats. The women spelled the men at the reins. The air chilled and Jabber pulled the quilts about himself and hunkered down next to Mama for warmth. Bessie walked beside the wagon, but there were few rocks to kick out of the way. The mountains to the north were jagged lines of starless black. The moon rose large and full, a blind eye that saw everything and nothing that crawled across the playa.

Bone weary men slumped in their seats, crusted and curling forward like tent stakes left in the ground.

Jabber sat a turn with Bessie as Pa slept. Jabber pulled the blankets about him and held the canteen to keep it warm. He counted the new freckles on Bessie's face, there was a dark one down on her chin, just below her lip. Her light eyes--blue in day--were colorless under the moon, and she stared--like Mrs. O'Fallon did--across the salt flat and beyond it.

A low hummock of earth rose up. The wagon rolled over it and down onto the salts again, then another rose, this one larger, like waves--waves of earth cresting and falling.

"Bessie," Jabber said.

Bessie stared, her head nodded on her neck like a ball.

"Bessie, Bessie look," Jabber said. He placed a hand on hers.

She started as if from sleep and yanked on the reins.

The oxen pulled up short.

"You see it?" Jabber asked.

"I see them," she said.

"What do you think they want?" Jabber asked.

A line of men and silent horses set on the terrace above. Dusted up and down with white they were and each one carried a rifle on his saddle.

No word, no warning, the first volley cracked through the night like thunder from ridge to ridge. Bessie screamed as she and Jabber tumbled backwards into the wagon.

The second volley ripped through the canvas, and Jabber put his hand in a pool of wet in the dark.

The men of the wagon train shouted. They circled back on each other, scrambling into a firing line.

"They ain't injuns," Jabber said.

Pa Walk hollered, "Get your rifles!" and he raised is gun, it's black barrel glinting in the dark.

Mamma groaned, lying on her side, her swollen belly wet and black.

"Mamma," Jabber said, as he crouched beside her.

She whispered a prayer with glassy eyes to the stars poring through a tear in the canvas.

Horses screamed, men howled and gunfire ripped across the hardpan like whip cracks, and then all fell silent.

Bessie lay against the blanket chest, her eyes wild and white. Jabber clutched Mamma's clammy hand then slipped over the side of the trap and scuttled under where Pa set up by the wagon wheel, his leg bandaged and a bullet between his teeth. The man looked worn beyond pain, but the fire was still in him.

"Go look after your Ma," Pa Walk mumbled with the bullet between his teeth as he pulled his boot on. Blood oozed out a hole in the side of it and stained the playa.

Pa sighed and leaned back against the wheel, popping the bullet out of his mouth and loading it into his rifle. "If they break the line, don't let'm find you here, you hear me? You go to your Ma and your sister. Promise me, Jasper."

Jabber nodded.

"Say the words, Jasper."

Jabber's lower lip quivered, "I pw'omise."

Pa smiled like it was the last thing he'd ever do and that smile turned into a grimace. He cupped the back of Jabber's head and said. "I would'a liked to see you grown into a man, but there ain't nothing for it now." Pa shouldered his rifle.

Jabber watched under the wagon, shadows of long legged beasts descended from the hills above like matchstick horrors from his dreams.

Jabber said nothing as he sat by his Pa and watched the night for monsters…and they came, oh they came silent in their gray and tan dusters. They came with their hats pulled down over their shining eyes with their rifles at their shoulders. They came crusted in salt and silt and stained with sweat and blood.

"You're trespassing," one of the riders hollered. "This here's Caleb land, and we're the sons of Caleb."

Mr. O'Fallon peaked over the edge of his trap. The mule lay dead beside him, it's legs already stiff. "We're heartily sorry about that, Sir," hollered Mr. O'Fallon. "We didn't know this land was spoke for. We'd be on our way off your land and cause you no more trouble if'n you would cease with the hostilities."

"Give up your rifles," the rider called. "And some of your stock. We'll call the insult settled."

"Insult my ass," Pa Walk muttered as he cocked his rifle. "They want our stock, they can come and get it."

Mr. O'Fallon waved for him to put it down. Pa Walk shook his head.

"Do we have your word," Mr. O'Fallon called out to the riders. "That our men, women and children shall come to no harm at the hands of you and your brothers?"

"That you do," The rider called. "Give up your rifles and stock and we'll escort you to the boarders of our land. Your arms will be waiting for you at Butcher's Ford, two days ride ahead. We don't want to see you, nor anymore of your kin crossing our land."

"We apologize, sir, again, a thousand times. We did not know," Mr. O'Fallon said in his lilting Irish tongue.

Pa Walk shook his head. "Opened up on us without word, without warning. No God-fearing man would ever--." A drip fell down from the trap, thick and red like molasses. Pa caught it on his finger and rubbed it against his thumb and smelled it. "Bessie?" he called.

"Pa, Mamma's hurt."

Pa looked to Jabber. "Jasper, go look after your Mamma. Do it."

Jabber scrambled up into the trap. Bessie leaned over their mother, holding her hand as Jabber slid between the clap-boards and canvas.

Bessie's pale eyes shimmered in the moonlight. "Jasper, I don't know what to do."

Blood pooled on the floorboards of the trap and their mother's face dewed with sweat.

Crunching, dragging in the gravel sounded beyond the canvas and Jabber saw Mr. O'Fallon's face briefly through a rip and Mr. Roland Coake was right behind him.

"We have to take their terms," Mr. Coake said.

"No," said Pa Walk, "They won't keep their word. You know they won't."

"I got Colleen to think of and she's barely hanging on," said Mr. O'Fallon. "Think about your girl, think about your wife."

Pa Walk said in a low even voice, "I am. They ain't gonna keep their word."

"I have to believe they will," Mr. Coake said. "When the sun comes up tomorrow, how long you think we're gonna last? May as well bargain now while we can."

Pa Walk shook his head.

Mr. Coake raised his pistol. "I ain't asking, Jacob."

"On your head be it," Pa Walk said, "but when they're laying us in our graves, may God have mercy on your souls, because they sure as well won't."

Mr. O'Fallon waved a white flag on the end of a shovel. The men of the wagon train--even Pa Walk--laid down their arms in a pile and the riders collected them. As dawn broke in the east, they lead the wagon train off the salt flats and into the sagebrush. They stopped there next to a draw.

Mamma Walk groaned and held her belly. "He's not moving anymore."

The riders lined up the menfolk along the dry creek bed.

"We are the sons of Caleb," said the lead rider. "And we don't suffer no slight."

They fired all in a line and the men of the wagon train fell into the draw.

Bessie's finger nails dug into the dry clap-boards. "Pa?" Her face blanched white. "Patrick?"

Lacy Coake screamed and ran towards the draw, her apron bloody, her hands cracked. She held her eldest boy, his blue eyes staring at vacant skies like one of Bessie's old dolls.

Colleen O'Fallon sat on the back of her trap, worrying her beads and praying to her Pope and all the saints, but not a one of them would raise her husband out of that crick bed.

The sons of Caleb walked from wagon to wagon, pulling the boys out where they found them--some no older than eight--and lined them up, despite the protests of their mothers and sisters and slit their throats to save the bullets.

They pulled Colby Roarke out of his mothers arms and marched him over to the draw. it was filled so high there wasn't enough dirt to hide the staring dead.

"He's just a baby!" his mother cried.

"How old is he?" one of the Calebs asked.

"He's seven," she said. "Please, he don't know you. Just let him be."

"The Lord will know his own," said the Caleb and slit the boy's throat from ear to ear and tossed him on the others.

grown into a man, but there ain't nothing for it now." Pa shouldered his rifle.

Jabber watched under the wagon, shadows of long legged beasts descended from the hills above like matchstick horrors from his dreams.

Jabber said nothing as he sat by his Pa and watched the night for monsters…and they came, oh they came silent in their gray and tan dusters. They came with their hats pulled down over their shining eyes with their rifles at their shoulders. They came crusted in salt and silt and stained with sweat and blood.

"You're trespassing," one of the riders hollered. "This here's Caleb land, and we're the sons of Caleb."

Mr. O'Fallon peaked over the edge of his trap. The mule lay dead beside him, it's legs already stiff. "We're heartily sorry about that, Sir," hollered Mr. O'Fallon. "We didn't know this land was spoke for. We'd be on our way off your land and cause you no more trouble if'n you would cease with the hostilities."

"Give up your rifles," the rider called. "And some of your stock. We'll call the insult settled."

"Insult my ass," Pa Walk muttered as he cocked his rifle. "They want our stock, they can come and get it."

Mr. O'Fallon waved for him to put it down. Pa Walk shook his head.

"Do we have your word," Mr. O'Fallon called out to the riders. "That our men, women and children shall come to no harm at the hands of you and your brothers?"

"That you do," The rider called. "Give up your rifles and stock and we'll escort you to the boarders of our land. Your arms will be waiting for you at Butcher's Ford, two days ride ahead. We don't want to see you, nor anymore of your kin crossing our land."

"We apologize, sir, again, a thousand times. We did not know," Mr. O'Fallon said in his lilting Irish tongue.

Pa Walk shook his head. "Opened up on us without word, without warning. No God-fearing man would ever--." A drip fell down from the trap, thick and red like molasses. Pa caught it on his finger and rubbed it against his thumb and smelled it. "Bessie?" he called.

"Pa, Mamma's hurt."

Pa looked to Jabber. "Jasper, go look after your Mamma. Do it."

Jabber scrambled up into the trap. Bessie leaned over their mother, holding her hand as Jabber slid between the clap-boards and canvas.

Bessie's pale eyes shimmered in the moonlight. "Jasper, I don't know what to do."

Blood pooled on the floorboards of the trap and their mother's face dewed with sweat.

Crunching, dragging in the gravel sounded beyond the canvas and Jabber saw Mr. O'Fallon's face briefly through a rip and Mr. Roland Coake was right behind him.

"We have to take their terms," Mr. Coake said.

"No," said Pa Walk, "They won't keep their word. You know they won't."

"I got Colleen to think of and she's barely hanging on," said Mr. O'Fallon. "Think about your girl, think about your wife."

Pa Walk said in a low even voice, "I am. They ain't gonna keep their word."

"I have to believe they will," Mr. Coake said. "When the sun comes up tomorrow, how long you think we're gonna last? May as well bargain now while we can."

Pa Walk shook his head.

Mr. Coake raised his pistol. "I ain't asking, Jacob."

"On your head be it," Pa Walk said, "but when they're laying us in our graves, may God have mercy on your souls, because they sure as well won't."

Mr. O'Fallon waved a white flag on the end of a shovel. The men of the wagon train--even Pa Walk--laid down their arms in a pile and the riders collected them. As dawn broke in the east, they lead the wagon train off the salt flats and into the sagebrush. They stopped there next to a draw.

Mamma Walk groaned and held her belly. "He's not moving anymore."

The riders lined up the menfolk along the dry creek bed.

"We are the sons of Caleb," said the lead rider. "And we don't suffer no slight."

They fired all in a line and the men of the wagon train fell into the draw.

Bessie's finger nails dug into the dry clap-boards. "Pa?" Her face blanched white. "Patrick?"

Lacy Coake screamed and ran towards the draw, her apron bloody, her hands cracked. She held her eldest boy, his blue eyes staring at vacant skies like one of Bessie's old dolls.

Colleen O'Fallon sat on the back of her trap, worrying her beads and praying to her Pope and all the saints, but not a one of them would raise her husband out of that crick bed.

The sons of Caleb walked from wagon to wagon, pulling the boys out where they found them--some no older than eight--and lined them up, despite the protests of their mothers and sisters and slit their throats to save the bullets.

They pulled Colby Roarke out of his mothers arms and marched him over to the draw. it was filled so high there wasn't enough dirt to hide the staring dead.

"He's just a baby!" his mother cried.

"How old is he?" one of the Calebs asked.

"He's seven," she said. "Please, he don't know you. Just let him be."

"The Lord will know his own," said the Caleb and slit the boy's throat from ear to ear and tossed him on the others.

Colleen prayed at the end of the trap, her beads flying through her fingers, staring--just staring--beyond all of them.

Three of the Calebs, all with hard, dark faces and sunken cheeks, leathery skin and wiry beards pulled back the canvas of the Walk trap to reveal Bessie, Jabber and Mamma.

Mamma's eyes stared skyward and a fly crawled across the lid. She didn't blink.

"Come on," the Calebs said as they pulled Jabber out by the suspender straps.

Jabber didn't say a word.

"Don't you dare!" Bessie shouted, standing up in the trap and stepping over Mamma to snatch Jabber back.

"How old is he?" One of the Calebs asked.

"He's six years old," she said, staring him straight in they eye, "and if you lay a hand to him, God will make such a place for you in hell that you'll wish you were lying by my father in that grave."

The Caleb looked to his brother Caleb, and there was little by which to distinguish them. The second Caleb addressed the boy, "What's your name, son?"

Jabber swayed from side to side, holding Bessie's hand and he wet himself.

"I said what's your name, boy?"

Jabber's mouth had forgotten words, the taste of biscuit dough and how to laugh.

The Calebs spared ten women of childbearing age and seven children. They brought the stock and their ill-gotten prisoners to a ramshackle adobe built around the remains of a Spanish mission. The old bell hung in the main square next to a stocks and a well facing the east. The bell was hung from an old ox yoke and when they arrived, Elijuah, oldest of the sons of Caleb, rang it three times.

Five women and a passel of dusty children appeared from the rabbit warren of low adobe doorways cordoned off by tattered horse blankets. Some were Indian women, their hair plaited down the sides of their high plained faces with hooked noses. Some where white and the children looked a mix of the Calebs and whatever dam that bore them. Here and there scuttled one with brown eyes and black hair, half starved and boney as a desert coyote.

From the old mission appeared a man, blind in one eye with yellow stains in his stubble beard, pushed in a chair by a girl with one blue eye and one brown. She looked some mix of white and Indian or Mexican, a comely girl starving on the edges of the desert. Her face bore streaks of dirt with no sign she ever smiled. The old man rose from his chair, peering at the gaggle of newcomers.

"We found them on the salts, Pa," said one of the Calebs.

"Fine mess you got there," said the old man. "Best set to divvying them up so you can take a man's ownership. Bring them before the well."

The sons of Caleb lined the women and children taken from the wagon train up between the well and the bell.

The old man hobbled by on a cane and inspected them.

"This one," he said, pointing to Colleen O'Fallon. "What's your name."

She stared at the sky, praying to her God.

"I said, what's your name," he yelled.

She muttered on, worrying her beads until he ripped them out of her hands. She spit in his face and cursed him up and down.

The old man backhanded her into the dust. "You ungrateful bitch," he said. "I could bring you into my family or leave you out here in the stocks, where all twenty-four of my sons could have his way with you then leave you to the desert. Do you want that?"

Colleen looked him dead in the eye, "God judgeth the Righteous, and God is angry with the Wicked every day."

The old man smiled, then he laughed, it was a hollow sucking laugh like wind over dry reeds. "Elijua Caleb. I give you this here woman to be your lawful wedded wife. Her new name is Ruth, Ruth Caleb, may she bear you many sons."

Elijuah pealed away from the twenty-four gathered riders. He had dark, almost black hair and blue-gray eyes. His face was pock marked and his beard close cropped. He wore a duster with blood stains and three holes in the breast. He looked like a younger version of the old man except half as crafty and twice as mean. He lead Colleen away on a rope into one of the blanket covered doorways.

Jabber flinched and turned into his sister's apron. Bessie held him and patted his back.

The old man moved down the line, his eyes passing over those beyond their flowering years and falling on the girls who were little more than children themselves. He selected out Mary Pershing who was fourteen in June. He picked Caroline Rove, and Margarate Coake who was thirteen. He gave them all new names and set them aside for himself, and then at last he came to Bessie.

"And what's your name, young lady?" He asked with a grin of yellowed teeth and rheumy eyes.

"Bessie Walk," she said.

"Your name is Charity Caleb," he said.

"The hell it is."

The grin vanished from his face. "Don't you sass me, girl or I'll have you whipped."

"Better'n being your bedwarmer."

"Jethro Caleb," he called.

A red-headed man pealed away from the now twenty lined up men along the front of the old mission.

"Yea, pa," he said.

"Take that boy there." The old man pointed at Jabber.

Bessie grabbed hold of Jabber by the back of his collar, "Don't you dare."

The old man smiled. "What's your name, girl?"

She glowered.

"Go on, what's your name?"

Bessie looked down at Jabber and then back at the old man. "Charity Caleb," she replied.

The old man said. "Jethro, cut out the heifer."

Jethro tossed Jabber to the side and grabbed Bessie by the braid and dragged her over to the others along the mission wall.

"The rest you gotta share," said the old man. Mary, Caroline, Margarate and Bessie walked before him into the old mission as the sons of Caleb drew lots for the rest. When it came to divide out the children, the sons of Caleb herded them around the well.

"What should we do with them?" Jethro Caleb asked as Elijuah emerged from the pueblo, tucking in his shirt tails.

"Keep'm," said Elijuah. "Keep them long enough to get a child on your wives."

"I don't want them," Jethro said. "What about you, Amos?"

Amos Caleb, a sandy-bearded boy of maybe nineteen shook his head. "Barely can feed my own as it is."

Elijuah looked them over. "Stick them in the pens," he said. "With the hogs."

The Calebs rounded on the children with their hands stretched out--some of them held whips and ropes and shaving straps--and the children of the wagon train, not one of them over six, save Jabber, with heads hung and eyes dry, marched towards the hog pens. One of Old Coake's grandson's took Jabber's hand. Jabber looked down at the boy, maybe two, maybe three. Jabber squeezed his hand back.

. . .

Jabber spoke no word since the day his father and mother died. He saw Bessie from a distance. If she spoke to him, Pa Caleb beat her. She'd smile at Jabber from across the well when she was getting water, but she always had tears in her eyes when she looked away. The mixed girl with the one light eye and one dark eye brought the children their slops--corn cobs, stale bread, moldy peppers and nopals, and the children fought the pigs for it. The little ones were the first to disappear. Some of them might have run for it, but they wouldn't have gotten far, not with the relentless sun beating overhead and desert for three days in every direction.

The Calebs lived by robbery and murder, they had no hand at farming--that was woman's work--and what food they came by was wagon rations, scrawny cattle and feral hogs.

Jabber marked Elijuah Caleb by the shadow he cast--darker and longer than the rest of his brothers. When the man walked out of his adobe, eyes followed him, the eyes of the women and his brothers, the eyes of the children that ran wild beyond the confines of the hog pen. He alone among his brothers would walk into the old mission with it's pigeons and crooked roof and consult with Pa Caleb, and when he emerged and gave the order to ride no one questioned him.

The weeks passed and Mrs. O'Fallon wouldn't bake, wouldn't eat, wouldn't do any of her wifely duties, no matter how much Elijuah beat her. She'd just sit there on the bench with a blanket over her head, staring off into the distance, her lips moving but no words coming out. Elijuah dragged her outside by the hair and tossed her before the stocks and said. "Woman, if you don't do as you're told," he drew his pistol and grabbed the little Coake boy by the ear and hauled him between the slats.

"No please," Margarate Coake cried as she ran across the courtyard.

Elijuah batted her away with his work hand and the gun went off. Margarate staggered away holding the side of her neck with blood spurting through her fingers. Screaming erupted through the courtyard as the women dropped their water buckets and ran to Margarate.

"Elijuah Caleb," Pa Caleb shouted from his chair as he wheeled into the courtyard with a twelve-guage slung across his lap.

Maragarate collapsed near the well, gasping and pressing her hand against the side of her neck. Bessie ran out of the mission with a stained towel in her hands and knelt before Margarate, pressing it to the wound.

"You're gonna be fine, Margarate, it ain't deep."

"It was an accident," said Elijuah Caleb, "she shouldn't have run up on me like that."

"You shot one of my wives, Elijuah Caleb. You lay down your gun."

"Pa, it was--."

The shotgun leapt to the old man's shoulder. "I said unpack yourself."

Elijuah raised his hands in the air slow and easy-like, with eyes ever on his father. He lowered the pistol and it fell to the earth.

Jethro and Amos leaned against the adobe walls of the warren and watched with hard faces.

Pa Caleb called. "Go on and take your brother to the stocks."

"Pa, it was an accident," Elijuah repeated.

"You can't rule your wife, and you done shot one of mine. You know the law."

Jethro picked up Elijuah's pistol and tucked it in his pants. He and Amos locked Elijuah into the stocks and cut the shirt from his back. Pa Caleb stood on shaking legs, but as soon as he had that whip in his hand, he was steady as a fence post. One, two, three lashes and the blood ran red from Elijuah's back. He did not scream. New gashes overlay old scars that crossed his skin like wagon ruts.

Margarate wheezed against the well and the blood ran down the right side of her gingham dress and all over Bessie's hands.

Elijuah set in the stocks three days and two nights.

Margarate lived out the week before the wound turned on her. They buried her behind the mission without a marker.

. . .

It was a month before Elijuah Caleb could sit a horse again. Jethro lead the posse when they went out riding with Amos as his second. The mixed eyed girl with the black hair and never-smiling-face saw to Elijuah while Colleen O'Fallon sat her days by the well, praying for the good Lord's deliverance. Every night, Jabber slept in the rafters above the hog barn, praying he didn't fall.

It was the end of summer, just before the rains came when Elijuah gave the order to ride and Jethro didn't mount up.

Elijuah stepped towards his brother. "I said we ride."

"I say different," said Jethro.

They stared at each other, all hard eyes and killing hands inches from their pistols.

"When I give the orders," said Elijuah, "that's the end of it."

Jethro sucked the air through the gaps in his teeth and mounted up. They road out just after dawn.

Bessie passed the hog pen on her way to the well. "Jasper, you in there?" she whispered.

Jabber eased up to the slats and stared through.

She stuffed a piece of cornbread through the slats. Jabber grabbed it before the hogs could smell it and he wolfed it down in two bites. He looked up at her for more, but there was none. She smiled with glossy eyes. Her cheeks were sinking and the skin on her hands pealed back from the splintered fingernails.

"We're going to get out of here, Jasper," she said. "Just stay alive and don't forget who you are, you're Jasper Walk--no matter what they call you, you're Jasper Walk and your father was a good man."

She scuttled away from the hog pen before the old man appeared in the courtyard with his wives and daughters behind him like a king. He surveyed the land, the chickens and the skinny mules, the few old horses lazing in the shadow of the mission.

That night, Jabber thought about what Bessie said and mouthed the words: I am Jabberwok.

The sons of Caleb returned at sunset two days later with Elijuah slung over a saddle and two bullets in his back.

"What happened?" Pa Caleb asked as they lead the remains in on a skinny pack-mule.

Jethro rode Elijuah's horse and sat in Elijuah's saddle. He leaned forward and spoke to the old man, "They got scouts, Pa. Saw us riding up. Shot Elijuah twice in the back like a dog."

Pa Caleb appraised Jethro then the body of his eldest boy. "Get him off that damn mule."

"You heard him, boys," Jethro hollered.

Amos and another brother yanked Elijuah's remains off the mule and laid him down in the dirt before the mission bell.

Pa Caleb looked him over and spit a stream of brown tobacco juice out the side of his mouth. A thin strand of drool glistened among his graying stubble.

Amos looked at his father and then at Jethro and said not a word.

The next morning, they buried Elijuah behind the mission where Pa Caleb said words that might have been a prayer and might not. He said them standing over the grave with his hat on his head as the flies hovered around the open hole. Elijuah lay uncoffined, his face purple and dry beneath the beard and the pockmarks.

They divided up Elijuahs possessions and Colleen O'Fallon went to Amos Caleb.

Weeks passed and Bessie snuck off to the hog-pens after dinner when the purple twilight grew long in the sage. She brought Jabber chunks of cornbread Pa Caleb hadn't eaten. Jabber tasted the old man--salt and tobacco--around the gnawed bit of gritty bread.

Bessie spoke. "I hid a water jug in the latrine behind the stables." She leaned in real close like she was tying her shoe and whispered. "We're getting out of here, Jasper, next time they ride out, we run."

Three days passed and two of the scouts came back from the range with news of a wagon train headed west across the salt flats. Jethro shaded his eyes against the red sun and spat into the dust. He looked at Amos and then out over the salts. "We ride," he said.

Twenty three brothers mounted up on skinny horses, their saddles cracked and worn. They road out as a crescent moon rose into the night.

Jabber waited at the slats as the last glimmer of lantern light vanished from the adobe. The half-breed girl waddled out of the old mission with a bucket of slops for the hogs. She tossed them into the stone baptismal-font sinking into the filth of the hog pen. Jabber waited until her back was turned and he slipped through the slat boards. He ran among the shadows until he reached the old latrine. Behind it, a small cache of rocks hid a water jug and a cracked purse filled with dried jalapenos and horse jerky.

Jabber waited. He waited a long time. The moon rose high across the desert and the salt flats glittered like ice. The hogs grunted in the pen. The adobe slept. Coyotes howled in the sage brush and somewhere out there, the sons of Caleb stalked the edges and ridges of the salt flats looking for wagons.

The gravel crunched under foot--bare foot. The sound was muffled and soft--a woman's foot, or a child's, and Jabber waited. He held his breath in the stink of the latrine. The gravel crunched again with hurried foot falls in the night. They reached the latrine door, but Jabber didn't look, didn't dare to turn.

"Jasper--Jasper, you there?"

Jabber peaked around the latrine and saw the shadow of a woman that might have been Bessie and might not.

"Say something if you're there, Jasper."

He opened his mouth, but no sound, no words came out. He kicked his heels into the gravel.

Bessie opened the latrine door but didn't go inside. She let it shut and slipped around the back on silent feet. "We gotta run, Jasper."

Jabber nodded. In the dark, he thought she smiled.

Bessie clasped his hand and they slipped off into the night.

They cut through the rocky edges between the salt and the sagebrush as the moon descended and the stars twisted in the heavens. Their breath hung white on the air, and Jabber shivered in his soiled shirt and tattered pants.

"So long as we're moving, we're gonna be ok," Bessie said.

Dawn broke in the east. The light spilled through a gap in the black mountains like rotten teeth rising from bleached bones. The winds kicked up and pelted them with sand and salt. Jabber shielded his eyes from it as Bessie dragged him onward--their feet cracked and bleeding.

They slept the day under a pile of sage brush during the hottest part. The branches smelled like medicine and cut his skin. He watched Bessie sleep for a while, her chest rising and falling under that torn and faded dress, and sometimes in her sleep, she held her belly.

The sun set and they pressed on, following the path of the moon as it cut across the night sky and endless desert and not a word passed between them. They reached the foothills of the black mountains where the ground was littered with sharp rocks and scorpions skittered among them. There they found a path, barely big enough for a snake, and they followed it among the rocks which were still warm to the touch.

Bessie stopped and drank a swig of the rancid water. She winced. "There'll be sweet water in the mountains," she said, handing him the jug.

Jabber drank.

The sun rose at their backs and they took refuge in a crack in the rocks. It widened as they passed through, opening up into a cavern the size of a small courtyard. As his eyes adjusted to the brown shadows, Jabber made out forms. He tugged on Bessie's arm and pointed. Bessie looked at them. She shoved Jabber behind her.

"Who are you?" she asked--her voice raspy and dry.

They did not answer. They just watched.

Bessie and the strangers stood there not speaking and Jabber hid behind her skirts. Bessie let go of his hand. Jabber clutched at it, yanking her back.

She removed his grubby fingers from her wrist and she approached the strangers. They wore blankets covered in salt and dust that looked to once have been horse blankets. One was a quilt made of mismatched bits of flannel. Bessie leaned over them.

"It's alright, Jasper, they're dead," her voice was a hollow reed, rasping agains the cavern wall. She motioned Jabber over.

He looked upon the dead--they had withered and didn't much look like people anymore and somehow that made it all right. Their gray skin pulled taught over the bones and it looked like they were smiling-- they must have gone to heaven.

Bessie pulled the blankets back. Jabber stepped away and shook his head.

"They don't need them anymore, we do," Bessie said.

Beneath the blankets, two more bodies lay curled against what would have been a woman in life. Her skirt was brown, the hem tattered and she wore no shoes. The children that curled next to her were small and stunted, one of them had dusty blonde hair. The adults were all women. Bessie rifled through their possessions. They didn't have much.

Jabber and Bessie slept beside the dead in the cave, and as night fell, they climbed among the rocks with the blankets wrapped around themselves. The water ran out half way up the climb.

"There's always springs in the mountains," Bessie said.

Jabber nodded and he kept on, his head hung low as he stumbled, one foot in front of the other through the rocks.

"I see a flat spot up ahead, we'll stop there and take a rest. Maybe there'll be water," Bessie panted and held her belly as she climbed.

They broke from the rocks with the moon over head and set foot on a bench of silt and sand. Bessie grabbed Jabber by the arm and hauled him up. They started crossing the mesa when in the quiet, a match struck. An orange glow briefly illuminated a man's face as he lit a cigarillo.

Bessie's shoulders sank, and her head hung.

Jabber clutched her wrist with both hands.

Amos Caleb hauled them back to the adobe on a rope. He presented Bessie to the old man before the mission. Abraham Caleb held the bullwhip in his hands, the unbleached leather cracked and stained with blood and skin. He spit a stream of tobacco juice into the dirt. Strings of spittle clung to his stubble chin, staining it yellow. The old man stood and in the adobe courtyard, his shadow was long and wavered in heat like it was laughing.

"Strip her," he said.

Amos pealed away from the wall and ripped the back of her dress open.

"Tie her to the post," said the old man, and his son obeyed.

Bessie fought him the whole way.

Abraham flicked the whip back like a sun serpent striking and it cracked across her back. She shrieked.

Jabber jumped.

Lash after lash the old man laid across her back like wagon ruts in the mud and she fell to her knees dry-heaving, gasping for breath.

"You gonna run out on your family? On your husband and sister wives?" the old man yelled and his voice echoed through the courtyard. "You belong to me. You all belong to me." Mary and Caroline stood there swaying from side to side. Caroline's hair was bleached bone white by the sun and it was brittle--fell out in clumps. Mary looked at the ground, anywhere that wasn't Bessie's bleeding back.

"Go on now, see to your sister," Pa Caleb said. The girls took Bessie down and brought her into the mission.

"What do you want to do with this one?" Amos asked, hoisting Jabber up by the suspenders.

The old man looked the boy up and down. "What do they call you, boy?"

Jabber didn't say a word.

"You answer me when I'm talking to you," the old man said, raising the whip, still wet with Bessie's blood.

Jabber wet himself.

"He don't talk," said Colleen O'Fallon. "Leave him be."

Amos turned around still holding Jabber in his hand like a scruffed dog.

Pa Caleb raised an eyebrow.

Amos dropped Jabber in the hog pens and took his wife back into the adobe.

The days crawled on into weeks, and Jabber didn't see Bessie. She didn't come out to dip water at the well, and sometimes he wondered if the old man had buried her in the night. Amos Caleb had no more luck with Colleen O'Fallon than his brother before him. He beat her and threatened, but all she did was sit on that bench and pray for the good Lord's justice. Amos' brothers laughed at him, said he couldn't rule his woman and so he went to the hog pens and pulled Jabber out of the rafters by his ankle and said, "You do what I tell you and you'll live, you hear me, boy?"

Jabber nodded without breathing and Amos lead him over to a low adobe hut that was little more than mudded over straw bales and clap-boards. Inside the hut, dogs lazed before the hearth--scrawny things the size of chickens--and the pups chased mice in the corners. A smoke hole in the ceiling let in the only light. One mud-brick bench along the wall served as a bed. It was covered in a bright mattress sewn of patchwork scraps of old coats and horse blankets and Colleen O'Fallon set there staring out that smoke hole, praying.

Jabber lived by the grace of Amos Caleb on the floor before the hearth with the dogs. He tended the chickens behind the adobe hut and mucked out the horse and mule stalls. He split fire wood with a ground-stone ax and dreamed of Lexington and the old porch where his father smoked after supper and Mamma sang as she washed up.

The mission village fell into routine. The women met at the well in the morning, and drew water for their daily chores. Maybe it was a sign from God, or maybe whatever had hold of her passed, but Colleen O'Fallon came back to the world of men. She would stand by the well at first with the rest of the women, drawing water. Soon she was grinding cornmeal and baking bread. Mary's belly began to swell, then Caroline's. The last children in the hog pen slowly disappeared into the filth.

Jabber prayed to the Lord to punish the Calebs for what they'd done.

In April, Caroline and Mary bore sons to Pa Caleb and Colleen was expecting her first child. While Amos was out ranging with his brothers, defending the Caleb lands, Jabber stayed home with Colleen O'Fallon and she'd talk to him sometimes and tell him stories. Sometimes she'd talk about Mr. O'Fallon and Boston and she'd cry.

The prairie bloomed with wild coneflowers, yellow daisies and white Star of Mornings and Jabber would pick bouquets for Colleen and put them in the cracked stoneware vase on the table when they'd eat their supper. He didn't see Bessie, not even in the mornings when the women went down to the well to dip water and he wondered if she ran without him.

It was over a month before Bessie returned to her duties of drawing water and grinding corn meal, and she walked with a limp. Jabber glimpsed her bare feet one day as she dipped water by the well, the two small toes on her left foot were gone. She didn't look at him again.

Jethro and the sons of Caleb road out weekly as the spring drew into summer, but the word had traveled along the wagon routs and the settlers traveled with hired guns. The posse came back minus a brother on the fifth of June. They left him where he fell and Jethro had a bullet graze on his neck. Amos inherited a second wife off his brother who died while defending the Caleb lands from the ever-present intruders cutting their way without a by or leave across the salt-flats from St. Louis. The girl came by name of Patience and she was a blonde thing, twenty if she was a day, with freckles on her upturned nose. She had two boys, four and six and they were cruel as the Caleb that sired them.

Amos moved his family into a bigger adobe near the mission that once belonged to Eli Caleb. It was a three room adobe with a small store room off the back. Colleen looked it up and down when she entered, holding her swollen belly.

"Stinks like dog piss," said Patience and she held her nose.

The women took to scrubbing the walls and the floors and Jabber carried water for them as Patience's children played with the dogs before the hearth.

Amos built bunks out of slat-boards and made beds for the children in the second room.

"You got some book learning to you, don't you," he said to Colleen.

She nodded.

"You're gonna teach them," he said, gesturing to the children.

"I don't want that crazy papist schooling my boys," said Patience.

Amos looked Colleen up and down. She held her belly and scowled at Patience.

"You teach'm to read and write," Amos said. "You can do that much, cain't you?"

Colleen nodded.

The children were all Caleb. They bit Colleen when she tried to teach them and threw stones at Jabber as he tended the chickens.

One hot afternoon in late June, as Patience cleaned the skillets with lye, the children caught one of the chickens behind the adobe and cut off it's toes. They tossed it into the air and let it run around the yard. It stumbled a few paces and fell, leaving bloody skids on dry earth. The boys laughed and threw rocks at it. They picked up the chicken and threw it in the air, watching it flutter as it fell to earth on it's bloody stumps.

Jabber did nothing.

When they'd tired of their game, they chased each other with sticks and whipped each other, laughing and cursing.

Jabber collected the chicken from the behind the adobe, he pet it's feathers. It's eyes were amber with black pin-head pupils that quivered in the afternoon sun. It didn't struggle in Jabber's hands and it made no sound. Jabber snapped it's neck and took it in to Patience.

"What on God's green earth did you do to that bird?" she asked, hands on her slender hips.

Jabber held the chicken out to her.

"Go and pluck it," she yelled, slapping him across the face with a wet spoon.

Jabber carried the bird carcass out side and sat on a bench beneath the kitchen window as he plucked and gutted it.

Patient's children ran past the bench, whipping each other's bare legs with mesquite switches.

Colleen sat at the long table in the kitchen, cutting the spines off nopals.

"Go fetch some milk for the boys," said Patience.

Colleen didn't look up.

"You hear me?" Patience asked.

The boys ran into the adobe, bruised and bloody and laughing. The youngest reached for the jar at Patience's elbow. She slapped his hand.

"That's poison," she said. "Poison, don't you hear? Don't you drink that."

The boy frowned and ran off after his brother into the second room.

"You," said Patience through the kitchen window, "Go fetch me some milk." She handed Jabber a tin pail.

Jabber wiped the blood on his pants and headed for the stables and milked one of the nanny goats. Some of the milk spilled on his hand. He licked it. It tasted gamey. Jabber brought the pail back to the house and Patience cooked it up on the stove as Colleen set beans out to dry above the hearth. Amos sat at the table, smoking.

The jar of lye was half empty.

The adobe woke in the small hours to screaming as Patience ran into the courtyard, tearing at her hair. Her boys--her beautiful boys--were dead, cold and dead and lying in their bunks with blisters on their lips.

Colleen was moved to the storeroom off the main house and there in the heat of July she gave birth to a girl-child, but it was sickly. The Patience fell pregnant again soon after the death of her boys and Colleen was all but forgotten. The baby girl lived out the summer but fell to coughing with the first chill and passed away sometime around harvest. Colleen cried like God Himself had told her there was no salvation, and she gave up praying at night.

One hot day in mid October, the Calebs caught a party stuck in the late rains out on the salts and relieved them of their horses, cattle and daughters.

Among them was a man come down from Provo with a camera box. Pa Caleb rounded up his sons with Jethro now leading the band of riders, and they set for a photograph. The man congratulated Pa Caleb on his fine, strong family, and was so complimentary of the old man that they let him go on his way.

Within a week, that picture appeared in the Deseret News accusing them of all manner of wicked deeds of which murder was paramount. The headlines showed artists renditions of the open graves where the bones of the dead lay bleached and picked clean by vultures and scattered by coyotes on open ground. There was a bounty on Pa Caleb's head for $2500.00 posted by a family back east and soon it wasn't just the lawmen looking for them anymore, but quick guns and Comanche trackers bread for killing.

Pa Caleb rounded up his sons and his favorite wives and they scattered like chaff on the wind. Some headed south down towards Mexico, others headed west and north towards Oregon Territory. When the man-trackers came to the mission, there wasn't a boy over twelve in the pueblos, but twelve was still old enough to hang.

Colleen walked into the stables one day and didn't come out again. Patience became the wife of another man. Bessie was gone, and Jabber snuck the old family bible out from under Pa Caleb's bed in the old mission, the one with the family tree that named every sour fruit spawned from his loins, and Jabber cut that picture from the Deseret News with all their faces marked and remembered and he set out to find them.

1887

   The sun is down and they are running. Behind them the burns remains of the trap and it's three passengers smolder orange in the din like a geyser to hell. Shadows move with eyes that flash like mirrors reflecting the evil of wicked souls. The heartless stars watch over all in dead and reticent silence as the light of brother suns released by fire returns to wander the endless cosmos and seek landfall on other planets less barbaric. Cinders and ash rise into the heavens and scatter across the hardpan like so much ticker-tape confetti stinking of burned meet, wool and hair. In the distance, the coulee beacons the bone weary horses and they stumble through the dark sniffing for it.

      Blenson's horse screams and reels at the strike of some snake unseen and unheard in the brush and they go tumbling down cursing. Blenson rises, gripping his shoulder. The mare shies away. The snake slithers off into the brush. Blenson takes his horse by the bridal, but already she limps and his left shoulder hangs down a little further than the right. He is dusted with ash and clay down the left side of his misshapen body as if he is already half ghost.

   Krikt pulls up short and turns back as Blenson tries to mount. The horse buckles beneath him. Her knee throws dark rivulets of blood down onto the white clays and he knows in that part of him that still prays at night, that she cannot hold a man.

Blenson shakes his head.

Krickt nods, pulls his pistol and shoots the mare.

She screams once, falls and does not rise again. Her blood shimmers black on the hardpan, reflecting the stars. The light recedes from her eyes. The pupils quiver and roll back into her skull.

Blenson retrieves his rifle and a box of cartridges. He leaves the rest.

Krickt hauls Blenson up, but his gelding complains and gets two spurs in his loins for his troubles.

They ride on until they reach the Columbia and take refuge in the timbered hills above. They light no campfires. No less than three of them keep watch till dawn with rifles across their laps and knives in their boots.

When the party wakes, one of the two Jaspers and the Oklahoman have disappeared. They've taken two of the packhorses, plus their own, and no doubt what they think is a fair share of the loot.

Krickt runs his fingers over the trail, feeling the earth between the hoof-prints and clicks his tongue disapprovingly.

Red Joe, who is by birth a Chapacaw, takes the reins of his paint pony and disappears along the trail without a word.

Jabberwok will not see him again for six days, and when he returns, he will be riding the Jasper's saddle and wearing the Oklahoman's ears.

...

The Marshall and his sons come to inspect the halo of hell that rises over the dry lake bed. As they approach, they find a black stain of ash upon the hard pan and pass it by like crow feathers scattered by the wind. They smell it before they see it, the stench of hair and singed flesh like meat fallen into the coals. The Marshall raises his kerchief against the stench. The buzzards and coyotes pick at what's left. Bits of pink meat bloom from the crusted black. The heads have popped open and the brains have bubbled out the seams. The dead were relieved of their belongings and the two women that were in the party with them. The Marshall hangs his head and says a prayer while his sons look on the carnage with hate in their eyes.

"We should go after them," says one.

"What of the women? Where are they?" says another.

"Most likely dead," replies the Marshall as he scratches the two day stubble growing at his chin.

The youngest son, Jeremiah, shades his eyes against the dust and white hot light of eastern sun. "There's only one halo, maybe they ain't dead." The other three look at him and he wonders if maybe that's not worse.

The Marshall urges his horse on and his sons follow after.

They find the women bloodied and naked wandering the wastes. Neither speaks nor cries or even shies at the sound of approaching horses and they regard each other with a mutual disgust once a canteen has passed between them.

Days pass, the Marshall and his sons scour the lonely places, and in this land there are many. They find human remains, eyeless and tongueless, nailed to a tree. All parts that would identify it as a man have been cut away or eaten. The skull grins malevolently from atop a hollow chest. Bears have taken the legs. Sap covers the shriveling head. Ants crawl across the cracked skin and carry away bits of flesh to feed their young. The scalp remains, but there are no ears, those have been severed by a blade.

...

Jabberwock rises. He opens the dog-eared bible and removes a yellowed clipping from the Deseret

News. He studies the last face and counts those he's crossed at twenty two.

Krickt sucks his teeth. His brow is long, set with two burning eyes neither green nor gray. Wisps of dusty-hair hang loose from a bandana. He stands. He surveys the plateau, watching the birds reel south like Moses before the Jordan. The sun hits the water and ripples gold towards the Dalles.

Jabberwok shades his eyes. If only it was true gold--more gold than any man, any hundred men, could spend in a lifetime. He looks down at the yellowed clipping. He pries a piece of bark off the log and carves the letters of the man's name into it. He spits on the name and throws the bark into the fire; watches it burn. The flames lick up the letters, the spit sizzles.

Krickt saddles his mount against the growing wind, "Git up," he calls to his men who gather around the remains of the fire.

Below, the valley wakes. Chapacaw canoes cross the river at Drewers Ford and cattle mill at the edge of the dry-wash.

Jabberwok saddles the colt and checks it's hooves.

The horse paws the earth and snorts.

"I said 'git up!'" hollers Krickt, kicking over the coffee pot.

The fire hisses.

The men swear and break camp.

In the distance, buzzards circle the plateau.

"We should head east," says Decker.

Krickt shakes his head. "No good, Orondo's east."

"South east," says Decker, "What you say, Jabberwok?"

Jabberwok looks at the scar on Decker's throat. He shades his eyes against the purple dawn and surveys the east side of the river. "Better north," says Jabberwok. "Up towards Ruby."

"We ain't miners," says Decker with a grin. He scratches the stubble skirting the scar on his throat.

"Don't nobody know that but us," says Jabberwok.

"We go north," says Krickt, sucking his teeth and that's the end of it.

Blenson raises a saddle onto the pack mule with one hand. His left arm swings limp and swollen.

The saddle tilts sideways as he cinches the girth. The mule brays and Blenson cusses.

Jabberwok rights the saddle and straps the mule for him and helps him mount.

They ride along the ridge, at the tree line. The trail narrows to a path and then disappears into the rocks. They drop into the trees, cutting north towards the coulee.   Blenson's arm is purple. His fingernails are white. "I need a doctor," he says.

Krickt studies him. "Can you move it?"

Blenson shifts on the pack mule. The arm doesn't move. Flies crawl across the shining skin.

"Ain't no doctor till Ruby," says Krickt.

Blenson grimaces. Sweat pours down his scalp and soaks the back of his shirt.

"It's my work-arm, Krickt."

...

They break from the trees south of Saddle Rock and water the horses at an abandoned homestead with three craggy apple trees and sagging farm house.

Jabberwok picks apples in sight of the camp.

The men laze on saddle blankets. Blenson squats by the stream, pouring water on his arm. The fingertips are black.

Beyond the stream in a field of golden oats, the house tilts towards the big river bend-- charred logs and slat rails chinked with prairie grasses and clay. Behind the house, stones engraved with dates and no names crowd among willow roots by a slat-rail fence.

Yellow sod clings to the roof in patches. The withered stalks of camas and cowslips creak and clatter in the hot breeze.

Jabberwok ducks inside the farm house. It smells of dust and decaying things. Darkness seeps in the corners. The carcass of a dog rattles in the wind whistling through the slat boards. Gray, dried, the dog's black lips curl away from yellow teeth and gray gums. It rests before the hearth. Jabberwok flips it over with his toes. It's ribs clatter and shake. Fly casings fall from it's belly.

Mice have had-at the bed. The straw litters the floor mixed with horse hair, cotton and black mouse droppings. In the hearth, the kettle remains; rusted and cracked--no good to any man.

Jabberwok leaves the farmhouse. The land beyond is gold and brown and black, the river is muddy and beyond it a dust cloud rises in the east.

Krickt sits a'horse on the ridge above--watching the river, watching the world with his cold eyes and crooked jaw. His head follows the dust cloud.

The men play cards in the shade along the stream and swap stories about men they've killed, women they've bedded and money they've lost.

Decker laughs and cracks a joke about a whore with two cunts.

Blenson washes his arm apart from the rest. Flies crawl across his back.

They travel within sight of the river for a day, then cut up a small drainage spilling out of the hills just south of a village of Yakimas and Wenatchiis. They trade for salmon and pemican with the axes and clothing they pulled off the ranchers in the trap. They follow the tributary north by northwest up into the high meadows beneath the snowpack. Yellow prairie opens up to green meadows and purple camas fields.

Deer graze along the path and a small heard of swamp elk crosses the creek.

They make camp at the tree line in a narrow defile with a creek.

Blenson leaves camp after dinner and sets in the rocks above the tree line.

The setting sun catches on the glacier and glows the fierce purple-orange of smithies forges that's too bright to look upon with the naked eye.

Coils of black bats filter into the night.

The mountains fade like iron cooling in the fire, straw yellow, rust red, then blue gray as the moon rises. Silver light pools in pockets above the trees where the late summer snows cling on the north slopes in avalanche chutes. Two deer, a doe and a buck, cross the snowfields, their black bodies throwing the shadows of monsters. A horned owl haws. A pica squeals.

Blenson fades into the sky, invisible but for a man shaped shadow against the snowfield. His legs dangle over the edge of a boulder as big as a stage coach, and it is small by comparison to the others. He sings to himself, a sort of lullaby. His left arm hangs limp in his lap.

Jabberwok stuffs his gun-belt under his bedroll.

The moon arcs above the mountains. It sets. The fire dies down to coals. Jabberwok pulls the blanket over himself. The night is for the dead, and they come to him. First his father, with hands outstretched, his shirt torn, his lips thin and wispy. Then his mother holding her round belly that curls and twists like she's carrying snakes. Her lips move but make no sound, the snakes coil down her legs and up her arms. Colleen comes last, Colleen with apron strings hanging round her neck and the dark circles under her eyes. They rise from the smoking coals and hover before him. Jabberwok fingers the old bible, and the white river he will never drink from wends across black heavens.

Krickt smokes by the fire, watching the night, watching the trees, watching the wolverine that sniffles at the snow where the deer walked across. Krickt rises. He walks into the trees. His footsteps die away. Jabberwok closes his eyes, he sees the name he carved into that piece of wood. A single gun shot rips through the valley. Jabberwok grabs his gun from under the bedroll and points it into the night. The others raise pistols and rifles. Decker holds a shotgun in one hand and a knife in the other.

No crickets. No wind. Just the clink of spurs and the soft tread of boots. Krickt returns.

"What's doing?" Decker asks, his shotgun trained at Krickt's head.

"Go back to sleep."

"Tell me what's done and I'll think about it."

Jabberwok counts the bed rolls. Blenson's is still tied to his saddle. Jabberwok lowers his gun. "We gonna burry him?"

Krickt sits at the fire and lights a cigaret on the coals. He sucks in a long draw and blows it out in one breath.

They break camp at dawn and saddle the horses. No one speaks. They descend the narrow trail in switchbacks, leading the stock. A streak of blood stains the boulder where Blenson sat. A raven lights on it. The bird preens and wipes its beak. It stares at Jabberwok with one amber eye. Two more birds, both black, maybe ravens, maybe vultures, circle above.

The posse follows the river north.

They come across a Wenatchi summer camp in the high meadows. They trade for salmon and salal pemican and offer a lady's handmirror and silver cigar case. Decker offers to buy a girl for three gold teeth he pried out of a Mormon. He is rebuked by the girl's grandfather. The Wenatchi ask for horses. Krickt won't part with a one. Decker offers the old man the mule. The old man refuses. Decker scratches himself and blows a kiss to the girl as they leave camp.

Red Joe catches up with them at mid day. He wears two new ears on his scapular of trophies. He's swapped saddles and stock. His old saddle is strapped to one of the pack horses and there's a doe slung across it, bleeding down the cracked leather.

That night they eat venison.

The next day Krickt, Jabberwok and Decker ride into Ruby.

Krikt buys supplies, cartridge shells, flour, coffee and tobacco. Jabber buys a hatchet and a length of rope.

"I'm looking for a one-eyed man by the name of Caleb," he says as the shop keeper takes his money.

"Don't know no Caleb," the shop keeper replies.

Krickt eyes Jabber before he leaves.

"He'd be an old man now," Jabber says to the shop keeper.

"How do you know he ain't dead?"

"He ain't dead."

"Might be," says the shop keeper. "Might have died years ago."

Jabber slaps the picture from the bible down on the counter.

The shop keeper flinches.

Jabber points to the face of Pa Caleb. "I'd be mighty obliged if you'd look at this man and tell me if you know him."

The shop keeper fidgets. "I said I don't know no Caleb."

"Just look at the picture."

The shop keeper's hands tremble as he glances at the photo. "Don't know him, sorry."

"You sure on that?" Jabber asks.

A bead of sweat runs down the side of the shop keeper's face. "What's he done?"

"Just answer the question."

"I ain't seen him, I'm sure."

Jabber tips his hat and leaves.

The shop keeper asks again as Jabber walks out the door, "What's he done?"

The dirt is dry underfoot and the air smells of sagebrush and drying hay. The river runs red with iron and three horses laze in the shadow of the post office. An old dog sleeps on the barber's porch under the window as grasshopper wings clap in the brush along the road. Jabber spits a stream of tobacco into the dry earth and crosses the street for the post office door.

Inside the clap-board building, Krickt seals up a letter and hands it to the mail clerk behind a grate.

"It'll be three cents to mail that to San Francisco," says the mail clerk.

Krickt puts three cents down on the counter. "How much for Juarez?" Krickt asks.

The clerk consults a piece of paper glued to the wall and adjusts his spectacles. "Seven."

Krickt folds up another letter and stuffs it into an envelope. He hands it to the clerk.

"You got kin down there?" the clerk asks.

Krickt leaves a nickel and two cents on the counter and walks out.

Decker appraises the posters on the back wall and thumbs the kerchief at his neck.

Jabber walks up to the mail clerk.

"Can I help you sir?" the man asks.

Jabber pulls out the old bible. "I'm looking for a man by the name of Abraham Caleb, though he might be going by a different name now."

"You boys bounty hunters?" the clerk asks, eyeing him.

"I'm going to show you a picture," says Jabberwok, "I'd like you to look at it, and tell me if you know the face."

The clerk nods.

Jabber pulls out the old picture and passes it under the grate. The clerk adjusts his spectacles and examines the photograph.

"Looks like…" he starts, then squints at the photo again.

Jabber's work hand clenches. "You know him?"

"Can't be sure," says the clerk, passing the photo back. "This man in some sort of trouble?"

"You seen him?" Jabber asks.

The clerk adjusts his feet, standing up to his full height. "Like I said, it looks like someone."

"That someone happen to be a one eyed man, an old man?"

"He do," says the clerk.

"He have a woman traveling with him--a half breed girl with two different colored eyes?"

"What's this man done?"

Jabber lays the photo between two pages in the bible.

"The girl run out on you or something?"

"You seen her?" Jabber asks.

The clerk adjusts his spectacles again. "There's an old miner up there in Smoke Canyon goes by the name of Isaac with a half-breed girl, comes down here every couple of weeks for the mail."

Jabber tips his hat.

Decker takes two-dozen handbills from the post office and they leave town.

Krickt leads, his hat set square on his head, his eyes peering southeast where the dust rises.

Jabber trails with the packhorse and looks across the sage brush down the long trough of the Okanogan. He spies four riders on dark horses setting at the ridge crest, casting long shadows against the rising sun. He watches them for a long time, their shadows shrinking. Might be scouts, might be Indians, might be sin itself.

Decker pulls out the handbills soon as he reaches camp. "O'Dell, you're worth an even fifty now."

O'Dell reaches for the hand bill and Decker snatches it away, saying, "I like wiping my ass on your face."

O'Dell laughs.

Decker reads through the bills as he hands them out. "You win, Krickt, $1500.00, as posted by Fort Lawton. Never did say what you did."

Krickt pulls his hat down over his eyes in the shade of a lodgepole pine.

"Joe, you're in third place with, looky here, $250. I never seen so much for a red man, mighty tempted to turn you in myself." Decker flashes his crooked teeth at Red Joe.

Joe sharpens his blade on a whetstone and spits on it.

"How bout that, Fowler? How you like being worth less than a red man?"

"Least I ain't heathen," says Fowler and he flicks a spent cartridge shell at Red Joe. Joe catches it in his left hand without looking up.

Decker thumbs through the handbills. "In second place, is yours truly at $750. Fowler, you're fourth with $210 offered by the Planchette family in Helena for…," Decker squints at the print on the bottom of the handbill, "I don't rightly know what that says, but it sounds bad."

"He had it coming," Fowler says as he pokes the fire with a scorched stick.

"Bolton, you're in fifth with $150. Arson."

Bolton strikes a match to his pipe and flicks the match at Fowler's beard.

Fowler swats it and swears. The air smells of burning fur and sulfur.

Bolton reaches into the pile. "Jabber, this you?" he asks as he holds up a handbill of a man, maybe twenty, maybe thirty, with hard eyes and a widows peak. "Kinda looks like you."

Jabber shrugs. "Kinda looks like you too."

Bolton squints at Jabber and then at the handbill. "I killed a few people in my day, but never no hanging judge in Yuma," says Bolton, "Some bad son-of-a-bitch if that is you."

"It ain't me," says Jabber.

"Sure looks like you though."

"I said it ain't me."

Bolton tosses the handbill back in the pile.

"Cavalry's riding north," says Krickt from under his hat. "Turned north when we did, and there's a couple of long shadows dogging our track."

"We should go South," says O'Dell.

"Naw, west, and head down the coast," says Decker. "We could make Mexico before the snows."

O'Dell's face puckers. "Mexico is South."

"So's Silver City from where we're standing," says Decker. "You wanna go back there, boy?"

Jabberwok opens the bible and stares at the picture. "I think we should keep heading north. Cavalry won't cross the boarder."

"To hell they won't," says Decker.

"We go north," says Krickt and no one argues.

. . .

The marshal and his sons track the party along the Wenatchi River and loose them again at the ford. The land is gold and brown for miles. The hills are soft like the curves of a woman lying under a cotton sheet. The river is a rocky band of silver running through the dust and wild grasses. Salmon shimmer through the wakes, red and gray and they scatter as the horses cross the river.

Jeremiah looks over the valley as they climb the ridge where the trees rise in thick bristle stands, and he spies a line of riders trailing a herd of naked ponies. "Pa, look there."

The marshal leans forward in his saddle, shading his eyes against the sun. "Cavalry," he says, "What the hell are they doing up here?"

His two older sons look at each other, their horses shake their reins and paw the earth.

A flash like a mirror lights upon the ridge above the valley to the east. The old marshal squints at it. It flashes again and the band of cavalry turn north.

"They ain't headed to Simcoe," says Jeremiah as the line of blue coats and black horses disappears around the gray cliffs at the river bend.

"That's no concern of ours," says the marshal and he rides up into the trees.

They cut for sign along the hillside and pick up tracks on a game trail below the crest. The marshal's oldest boy jumps down and feels the hoof prints.

"Iron shod," he says. "Big. These weren't ponies."

The marshall nods. "Probably our boys."

They follow the trail up a rocky defile and lead the horses as they climb on foot. Vultures circle overhead and the smell of spoiled meat wafts down from the scarp and leaves the taste of rotten eggs on the palate. A streak of blood marks a boulder and the flies hum in a choir over the spot. Jeremiah hands his reins off to his brothers as they reach a bald patch with sandy soil and stunted trees. The marshal feels the earth and rocks of the fire pit.

Jeremiah climbs among the boulders in the scree and he hears things below him fighting, and the tearing of cloth. Ravens and red-faced vultures light on the rocks like mourners in boot blacking.

"This one didn't make it," Jeremiah calls.

His brothers join him, climbing the rocks hand over hand, and look down through the boulders and see the soiled remains of a shirt, a clump of hair hanging on a flap of scalp, a skull with one eye sunk back into it's socket. The body jerks and flops. Snarls rumble from beneath. The flesh ruptures and thick brown blood oozes from the shoulder; the arm disappears into the darkness and the brothers hold their breath.

They saddle up. The marshal and his sons follow the trail at the tree line and over three drainages shunting rivers off the white mountains rising like gods of the old land to the north. And there, among the trees smoke rises. Large black billows hang above the white snow pack, and the trail points to it like an accusing finger. They keep to the tree line, cutting through low passes and descend into a meadow where the smoke hangs woolen in the trees. The remains of a Wenatchi summer camp, poles from ten tipis maybe more, smolder in five bonfires and the dead lay scattered and unburied. Jeremiah crosses himself as he walks among the slaughtered, the old, the young, the strong, the infirm, the killers spared none.

The marshall inspects the line of the dead, fanning out in an arc and shakes his head, muttering under his breath and spies a boy watching from the trees.

The marshal raises his right hand and then his left, palms empty and facing the boy, but the child runs into the trees.

"They aren't all shot," says his oldest son. "Some of them look like they were cut down."

"Our boys didn't do this," says the marshal.

"Should we burry them?" Jeremiah asks.

The marshal mounts up and his sons fall in line, but Jeremiah terries over the corpse of an old man, slit from stomach to sternum and in his wrinkled hand he holds a lady's hand mirror.

The marshal and his sons follow the river and a horse trail where the riders traveled three abreast and obliterated the track beneath. The trail splits in two when they hit the Chihuahua.

   "Don't want no fancy work, you hear," says the Marshall to his eldest sons. "You see them, you send up sign."

   They nod.

   "I want your word," the marshall says.

   "We're just gonna find them," says the oldest son. "Then we'll send up sign."

The marshal and Jeremiah go up Roaring Creek and the two older sons follow the Chihuahua track back towards the Wenatchi River, east as the moon rises.

. . .

   Krickt keeps to the trees and the men follow. They travel under the ashen light of a waning crescent moon, and there are no signs this land was ever touched by the hand of man or hoof of cattle. Cliffs rise on either side of the valley, sliced out of the living rock. The posse reaches the confluence at the overflow where camp fires blaze above the ford.

   "I don't want to see so much as a match struck," says Krickt.

They wrap the tack and stow their spurs and turn up river within sight of the cavalry and Colonel Haller is none the wiser when they pass within one-hundred feet of his tent.

They cut along a goat trail rising from the river flow, switch-backing along a granite wall. The mule slips in the sand and goes over screaming, taking the pack horses with it.

The posse reaches the top where a black lake beckons like blood pooling in the earth.

Decker sleeps on his saddle, snoring as the mosquitoes buzz around his stubble beard. O'Dell crouches, curled in the roots of a fir tree, clenching and unclenching the hilt of his knife.

Jabberwok removes the old bible, he thumbs through the pages at random and his finger lights on a passage, it reads: God judgeth the righteous, and God is angry with the wicked every day.

Jabber glances to Decker who swats mosquitos with his meaty hands as they hover at the shiny scar at his throat. Red Joe's obsidian eyes peer above the scapular of ears. Fowler stares into the fire where the flames dance orange and pink up an old spruce log.

Fowler's lips move as if in prayer, and he whispers, "The son of a bitch had it coming." Bolton stares at the fire with the face of a boy watching a woman undress for the first time, his eyes leap with the flames and a smile plays at the corners of his mouth. Krickt watches the stars with his hands behind his head and his gun stowed beneath his saddle. Jabber turns to the picture in the old bible and the last blurry face. He closes the bible and stares up to heaven and the stars where once Bessie said Jesus lived. Jabber whispers to the night, "ain't nothing for it."

. . .

The sun rises and they eat shriveled salal berries off the game trails and follow Red Joe through the vine maple and scree and drop down into a slot canyon where the stone roils like water in streaks of gray and ash and black as if God himself once laid a hand to this land and burnt it before the flood. Jabber makes a game of picking forms and faces among the swirls like clouds of smoke rising from the river--here a serpent ready to strike an ankle, there a child reaching for a pear. The canyon narrows as they ride up it, in some spots the walls at the top are so close they nearly touch.

"We got to get out of this canyon," says O'Dell, "I don't like it. Feels--feels like."
"Like what?" asks Bolton.
"Like riding up the devil's asshole, that's what," says O'Dell.
Bolton puckers his lips and makes kisses at O'Dell.
A rock fall ahead clatters into the canyon.
Krickt stops and looks at the escarpment. His right hand grazes the butt of his pistol. Nothing moves,

and in the dark, no shadow rises. He walks on. Jabber sloshes through the water and catches up.

"Ain't far now," he says.

Krickt nods. The hand stays at his pistol.

The sun sets and the the canyon darkens in shades of red mixing with the gray and the black. Cold-fire eyes watch them from the rocks.

"Don't like it," says Decker. "We ain't headed north no more, we're headed back west, where we come from."

"It's just till we get to the road," says Jabber.

"What road?" asks Decker.

"The Smoke Road. Leads up out of the canyon," says Jabber.

"You better pray to God you're right," says Decker, "Cause if you ain't, I won't be riding to hell alone."

Bolton mutters something under his breath.

Jabber touches the worn bible in his saddle bags.

They ride until the last ashen rays of the setting moon glance across the cliff tops and skirt a dry creek bed up a narrow road, barely big enough for a man.

Krickt stops and glances up the defile. His horse paws the earth and snorts. They terry in silence, listening to the night. No wind cuts down the canyon. Mosquitoes buzz about their heads. The night smells of stagnant water, of dust and coyote urine. Krickt starts up the road, slow and quiet. The others fall in behind him. No one speaks, and not a man of them has a hand off his pistol.

Three miles they walk the horses and in the distance a light glimmers, faint and orange like a firefly growing ever larger as they approach. Jabber dismounts.

"Where you going?" Decker asks.

"I don't fancy sleeping out here tonight," Jabber says, "do you?"

Decker looks to Krickt.

Krickt sucks his teeth and looks at the light shining through a oil paper window. "And if it ain't him?"

Jabber looks up at Krickt as he hands him the reins. His face is that of a man, but filled with a hate only known to children.

Krickt nods. "So be it."

Jabber walks up the gravel trail to the old shack made of bits of dead trees, waddle and daub covered with a tarpaper roof.

Jabber knocks on the door. Someone moves inside. Jabber steps to the side, drawing his pistol but keeps it low.

"Who's there?" an old man calls.

"I'm looking for a man called Isaac," Jabber says.

"Who's looking?" says the old man.

"My name is Ephraim," says Jabberwok, "Ephraim Caleb."

No coyotes howl in the distance, no crickets sing in the rocks, and nothing moves inside that tar-paper shack.

"Ephraim?" says the old man. "Don't know no Ephraim."

"Maybe you knew my mother, Charity--Charity Caleb?" Jabber calls.

"Charity?" The old man's voice quavers on the still air. "Why don't you come in out of the cold there, son. The door ain't locked."

Jabber holsters his gun and pushes the door open with his left hand.

The old man sits at the table, his hair streaming about him in dirty streaks of yellow white. His stubble beard is caked with food and filth and stained down the left side with tobacco juice. The man looks like Pa Caleb, but then all old men start to looking the same after a certain age. His face is haggard, his cheeks sunken, his one good eye is dark, the other one is leached of color.

"You said you was an Ephraim Caleb?" the old man asks.

Jabber nods.

"Come closer," says the old man, "I cain't see so good."

Jabber scans the small room for the girl, but she's nowhere to be seen. He steps into the lamp light.

"You come all the way out here to find me, boy?"

"I did, sir," Jabber replies.

"On account you think I knew your mother? That's a long way to come."

"Didn't say where I was coming from," Jabber replies.

The old man smiles over black and crooked teeth, "That you didn't…that you didn't. Closest town is Ruby and that's a three day ride."

"Two and a half," says Jabber as he fingers the butt of his gun under the table.

"How is your mother?" the old man asks.

"I was hoping you could tell me."

"Why'd you really come out here, son?"

"She's dead, isn't she?" Jabber asks.

"I don't know."

"Are you Abraham Caleb?"

"I don't know no Calebs," the old man replies, staring across the table, that little smile playing at the corner of his mouth, the other corner drooling.

"Maybe your girl knows."

"I ain't got a girl."

"Folks in Ruby say different."

"Folks in Ruby don't know shit."

"I'd like to talk to her."

"Well you can't, she died."

"Show me where you buried her," Jabber says. "Go on, get up."

"I'm an old man, I'm gonna die out here alone."

"Not if I kill you you ain't. Go on, get up."

The old man shakes as he rises from the table. His back is bent and his arms are thin and covered with bruises.

Jabber grabs the lantern off the table and follows behind the old man out into the night.

The old man stumbles in the dark, grasping at boulders.

He points to a rocky overhang. "There," he says. "Go have a look for yourself."

Jabber cocks his pistol. "I'm gonna ask you one more time, are you Abraham Caleb?" "No."

"I was gonna kill you anyway."

"Then it don't make no difference who I am."

"You got anything you want to confess?"

"I don't know what happened to your mother, honest."

"She wasn't my mother."

"I done wrong in my life, but never to no woman named Charity."

"Her name was Bessie before you took it from her."

The old man sobs. "I never done what you think I done."

Jabber raises his pistol to the back of the old man's head. "They're all dead. All twenty-four of your sons. You're the last one."

The old man's sobs turn into laughter.

Jabber pulls the trigger. The shot echoes through the canyon and the laughing stops.

...

It's noon before the marshal's sons ride into Ruby. The eldest stops at the post office, the middle son checks the general store.

"Deputy," the mail says and clerk tips his visor as the marshal's son walks in.

"Did a posse come through here yesterday or the day before?" the marshal's oldest boy asks.

"Posse? No, but we had three men come through here day before last. One of them posted two letters."

"Do you still have the letters?" The clerk shakes his head. "Mail went out this morning."

"You know where they were headed?"

"What have they done?" the clerk asks.

"Murder."

The clerk drops his gaze, "I thought they was bounty men. One of them asked after a one-eyed old man. Showed me a picture."

"This old man live round these parts?"

"He's a hold up in Smoke Canyon," says the clerk.

The marshal's sons meet in the street before the vacant courthouse and leave a letter for their father at the post office before they ride out. The sun is low in the sky when they reach the ford where the sand is cut up with hoof prints and burn scars from cooking fires.

A broken wheel leans against a tree and the heavy ruts of artillery wagons cut north.

"Mail clerk says they've gone up Smoke Canyon," says the older brother

"Tight squeeze in there," says the younger. "We should wait for Pa and Jeremiah."

"We do that and they'll be over the boarder."

"Maybe."

"What you mean 'maybe' it's a three day's ride, we'd never catch them," says the younger.

"Smoke Creek dumps into the Similkameen south of Chopaka peak."

The younger brother says, "That's right on the boarder."

The older brother nods. "But not across it."

They ride towards Nighthawk and reach Loomis before sundown. They sleep rough on the shores of the lake, counting constellations like when they were boys. They eat a supper of salt beef and beans and tell stories to the roar of the Similkameen in the distance.

...

Krickt rises before the sun. His men raid the old man's coffee and stores in a mine shaft below the floor boards. He didn't have much, a quart of molasses, three cups of wormy oats, some kerosene and a worn saddle with a broken pommel. They find the horse--or what was left of it--further down the shaft, hanging from a cross beam. He'd been eating it for a while. It had been a boney creature in life. Maggots crawl in it's mouth and eyes.

They ride out at dawn in the shadow of Chopaka Mountain, with the snows still shining on her shoulders like an old woman's white hair. The road is little more than a trail and it stinks of goat urine and cuts back north again. They come to a wide spot in the canyon and along the walls, pictures of lanky figures--long legged men or spirits with thirteen ribs and heads like the fleshless skulls of dogs or coyotes--are pecked into the rock. Red Joe looks at them. He looks at them for a long time as the others file past him. Fowler picks up a rock the size of a cannon ball and throws it at the carvings as hard as he can. The edges of the relief chip and shatter, and fall to earth to join the sands.

"Fucking heathen," says Fowler as he picks up another rock.

Red Joe pulls a knife.

Fowler throws the rock at Joe.

Joe drops into the dirt and Fowler smiles.

Joe stands and brushes the sand from his shirt. There's blood seeping down his left pant-leg.

"Quit the bullshit," says Jabber.

"He drew on me," Fowler replies.

"You're a son-of-a-bitch, Fowler," Bolton says.

They mount up again once the road widens. The trail is littered in schist that flashes red with garnets like blood drops on the ground. Bolton and Jabber ride between Joe and Fowler. Joe watches Fowler's back with his dark eyes and says nothing.

The road cuts up out of the canyon as the white water rages below them towards the Similkameen. The sun is high and hot. The schist flakes off in knife blades. The horses hooves bleed. They reach the confluence of Chopaka creek and the Smoke, four hours ride from the border and a gunshot rips across the canyon.

Bolton's horse goes down, pitching him into the white water. He screams once before he's sucked under.

Fowler draws, but he's not fast enough. A knife grazes past Jabber's ear and sticks in Fowler's face, just below his left eye. He slumps in his saddle. His hand raises and he paws at the hilt. He pulls the knife out of his face and a stream of blood and yellow fluid drains down the front of him. His fingers twitch and his gun falls from his hand.

Decker draws on Joe just as another shot rings out across the canyon and strikes the rock wall behind him. He looks up. A mirror flash lights on the cliffs above.

"SCOUTS!" Decker yells.

They turn, Joe leads. They drop back down into Smoke Canyon.

Jabber and Krickt run at the back. Jabber unloads on the spot where the mirror flashed with both pistols.

Krickt raises his Remmington. He aims. His hands are steady, his breathing calm. He fires. The mirror flashes again, and the form of a man falls from the cliff tops and down into the white waters. He floats face up, arms out, legs splayed in the eddies between two boulders. He wears a dark blue jacket with horn buttons and buckskin gloves.

"Cavalry," says Krickt, "Haller's, probably."

Jabber nods.

They turn back down into Smoke Canyon. Krickt calls up to Joe, "Any other way out of here, Joe?"

Joe nods and points to Chopaka peak.

"Shit," says Decker. "Jabber, you and me are gonna have words when we get out of this."

Joe leads them up a game trail into the high country. There's no tree cover, just boulders and thistles. They pass within sight of a herd of mountain goats, cropping the grasses along a steep incline. Jabber leans forward in his saddle as they climb up the cracked granite and the schist. They come to a col between the shoulders of the mountain and they keep their eyes on the rocks. A shadow passes over. Jabber looks up. A raven soars above their heads, circles back and lands on a boulder the size of a house. It watches them with golden eyes and a shining beak as they pass beneath. O'Dell crosses himself. The raven caws once and flies away. It lights on another boulder some thirty feet up the escarpment. Krickt eyes the bird. He sucks his teeth and that Remmington is at his shoulder. He fires. A horse screams. The raven flutters it's dark wings and bobs it's head cawing. Krickt fires again. A man runs through the rocks, picking his way like a marmot. Krickt fires. The man falls and crimson blooms from his shoulder. He scrambles, falling on his backside and pulls a pistol. He fires. The shot goes wide. Another man appears from the rocks, his coat is gray and dusty. He grabs the second man and pulls him under cover. The two men burst from the boulders on the back of a dapple gray--a stocky mountain horse with a dark mane and white socks.

That mountain horse strains up the scree, his nostrils flaring, his mouth foaming.

The man on the back of the saddle reels. His blood stains his gray coat. It stains the horse's flank, and he's still firing as the other reins the horse up the goat trail.

The wounded man falls off the back of the horse.

Krickt raises his rifle and leads the horse and rider. He closes his left eye. He fires. The man falls from the horse into the rocks.

"Get the pony," says Krickt.

Jabber and Decker ride up into the rocks. They track the wounded man among them, his blood stains the gray granite in smeared handprints and drips that turn the white gravel pink.

Jabber rounds a boulder, his pistol in his hand. A man is lying on the ground, his eyes staring skyward. His chest neither rises nor falls, and the blood seeps out of him into the sand. A pistol lies inches from his outstretched fingers, a colt. Jabber takes it and stuffs it in his belt. On the man's chest he sees a tin star. He leaves it.

Decker rifles the man's pockets. He takes the watch and the money. They follow the dapple gray and come across the second man lying in the damp sand. He raises his pistol and fires. The bullet strikes the rock next to Jabber's head and ricochet's into Decker. The bullet grazes Decker's ear and the rock chips slice into Jabber's cheek. Jabber shoots the man in the stomach. The man drops his pistol, but lives.

Krickt keeps that rifle at his shoulder and watches the boulders above.

Decker swears and draws his knife.

"Leave him," says Jabberwok.

Decker leans over the man and gets to work.

Jabber turns away, but the sound follows him.

He catches the horse in a stand of heather. Below him, line upon line of white cavalry tents billow in the wind and the dark shapes of scouts slink among the rocks. The sky darkens. Jabber returns. The man he shot is dead and the corpse is mutilated. Gray thunderheads gather in the north and lightning flashes along the mountains.

Jabber brings the horse down and hands it off to O'Dell. Decker ties up his ear with a kerchief and pulls a tin star from his shirt pocket and tosses it to Krickt.

Krickt inspects the star and sticks it in his saddlebags.

Decker tucks his trophies into the grubby front pocket of his duster.

Ravens hop among the rocks where the blood seeps.

"The cavalry's camped along the Similkameen, there's scouts up every tributary," Jabber says.

"You saw it?" O'Dell asks.

Jabber nods.

"It was your fucking idea to come up here, Jabberwok," says O'Dell. The dapple gray throws it's head and he yanks on the reins.

"Ain't nothing for it now," says Krickt. "Joe, find us a path."

Joe leads them over the pass and up a ridge around the head of a clear tarn lake. The storm is upon them as they start down the ridge spur. The rain falls cold and heavy, the sky is dark gray, almost green.

The horses throw their heads and roll their eyes with each crack of thunder. They ride on until the darkness comes and they're soaked through and shivering but they reach the crest of the last ridge--a sharp ridge, a long ridge, a ridge that stretches for miles across the boarder. The rocks are slick and the horses stumble onwards. A lightning fork pierces the dusk with a red glow and the green blackness returns. They lean back in their saddles and they start down the spur towards a bald promontory. The lightning flashes again, and a man stands in their path. He stands on the bald rock of the promontory. Wisps of dirty white hair flutter around his sunken face, but his eyes burn with that same red fire that lights up the dark.

"Jasper Walk," he calls. "I've been waiting for you."

Jabber stops, frozen in his saddle.

Decker raises a pistol. Krickt raises a hand. O'Dell and Joe look on with wide eyes.

"Friend of your's, Jabber?" Decker asks.

Jabber shakes his head. He keeps shaking his head.

"Mister, we ain't got no quarrel with you," says Krickt.

The old man laughs, it's a dry laugh, a sucking laugh and says. "Captain Llewellyn Kriechton, you killed your father at the age of twelve."

Krickt lowers his hand and he stares at the old man.

Decker clicks the safety off, "I killed my first man at seventeen and I ain't afraid of you." Decker fires three rounds. The bullets pass through the old man and leave no mark.

The old man laughs again, that terrible laugh ringing through the rocks like an iron bell. "It's time to come home, boys."

The sky opens up above them, swirling flames descend like the red autumn leaves. The forms come together, twisting and flickering. Great red steers with gleaming horns bear down upon the mountain. Decker screams, impaled on the horns of a maddened bull as it drags him across the shale. The wisps of ash that were once Decker are beaten away by the wind. The bull throws it's head, the muscles of it's neck undulate, revealing the forms and faces of men-- thousands of men, their mouths twisted in agony their muscles burning--burning never to know rest, never to know sleep, never to know peace as they race across the endless skies.

O'Dell's horse bolts, and falls over the edge. O'Dell yells, the horse screams, and they are swept away in a river of fire. Red Joe is cast under and dragged across the night in a pillar of flame that coils up into the clouds like twining serpents, one trying to devour the other. The riders come, neck and neck on bone-weary horses at full gallop drawing whips of fire. Krickt and Jabber stand apart as the river rages 'round. Riders descend from the clouds, their whips curl around Krickt's throat and Jabbers ankle and the two are dragged, man and horse into the burning sky.

. . .

In the Similkameen valley, the cavalry tents buck and tear at their tethers as the rain and the hail beats the camp sideways. The river swells. The horses scream and rear; some break free, running into the unnatural night. The clouds crash upon each other in waves to gird the mountain, roiling with faces and mouths and eyes and some among the cavalry cross themselves and mutter prayers in the name of Christ.

Along a jagged rib of rock stretching north across the border, a sunset redness gathers. It spits forks of lightning off boulder and spire, shattering the rock and blackening the stone. Shards fly like birds caught upon the wind and are carried far before they slice into the earth.

The marshal and Jeremiah reach Colonel Haller's camp to find men chasing horses and tents torn to shreds. The scouts return with cuts on their faces and one man is blind.

The marshall turns to his son, "Stay here."

"I'm coming with you Pa," Jeremiah says.

The marshal shakes his head. "Not in this."

"You're a fool," Haller calls from his tent. "There's fire on the mountain. Up where there ain't nothing to burn."

"I'm a father," the marshall calls back, "and my boys are up there."

The marshall starts up the Smoke Road.

It is the last time that Jeremiah will see him.

1897

Dawes sits in his saddle, leaning forward with the spy-glass shaking in his hands.

"Do you see it?" Benchley asks.

"I don't see shit," says Dawes, "Wait."

A dust plume rises along the road to the north.

"It's a comin," says Dawes.

Benchley yips and he tightens his rawhide reins.

"You wait for the goddamn signal or I swear to Jesus I'll have your balls," says Pratchet.

Benchley glares at him, "Fuck you, you old coot."

Pratchet spits a stream of red tinged chew in front Benchley's horse, "Boy, only thing you know about a broken down old man is he's outlived all the idjits," Pratchet says and he smiles. "Hundred bucks says I outlive you."

Benchley laughs as his horse throws it's head, "I'm gonna shit on your grave, Tom Pratchet."

"You look mighty pretty in those feathers and beads," says DeWitt, making kissing sounds at Benchley.

"Remind you of your sister?" Benchley asks.

DeWitt scowls, it's an uneven, slow faced-scowl like a potato left too long in the earth.

Dawes raises his hand. His horse paws the sand.

Dust rises from the valley, and the sound of hooves thunders past the box canyon.

"Now," says Dawes.

Yipping and hollering, they all tear out of the canyon. They fire their guns, screaming like all the devils of hell were riding their shoulders.

The mail coach kicks up a cloud of dust so thick the shot-gunner fires blindly from the stage coach.

Pratchet falls back when they reach the river Y.

Dewitt stops behind him.

Benchley keeps going.

Screams erupt from the stage coach horses as they fall on bloody hooves. The coach teeters. The shotgunner bails as the driver hauls back on the reins. The coach crashes into the river.

Benchley whoops and hollers as he rides up on the wreckage, gun raised like the hand of God, his face painted white and yellow with clay.

His horse rears, shrieking and throws him into the earth. She limps away, a caltrop sticking from her left front hoof and the sweat shining on her auburn flanks. Benchley lies winded on the earth as the others ride up.

"What did I say?" Dawes asks. "What did I fucking say?"

Benchley tries to answer, he's winded and there's something stuck in his back.

"We stop before the fucking Y, because?" asks Dawes as he reloads his revolver.

Benchley gasps for breath as warm wetness seeps out of his back.

Wounded horses thrash in the river. Some are already drowned. A man's body lies face down in the shallows, his hat floating down river. Blood tinges the water pink.

Dawes shoot's Benchley's horse in the head as she staggers along the road. She crumples forward, her head driving into the earth. He hands the saddle bags to Pratchet. "Go on, grandpa," he says.

Pratchet grumbles as he staggers into the water on stiff, bow-legs. "He's your fucking shitheel cousin," he yells back at Dawes as they pull the bags of the mail wagon. "Aught to be you down here."

They stuff everything they can into the saddle bags and let the rest float down the river.

Dawes stands over Benchley and lights a cigarillo. "Get up," he says.

Benchley pushes himself up with his good arm, the other one's gone dead cold. The ground beneath him is wet and warm like he pissed himself.

Dawes looks at the red stain beneath his cousin. "Shit."

DeWitt and Pratchet load up their horses.

"Oh fuck," says DeWitt as he eyes the blood leaking out of the sucking hole in Benchley's back.

"Can't leave him, they'll know it wasn't injuns if we leave him," says Pratchet.

"Have to," says Dawes, "He'll slow us down."

"Well I ain't doing it," says DeWitt.

Dawes looks at him, "He's my fucking kin, the two of you flip for it."

Pratchet grumbles to himself as he pulls a shotgun from his saddle. He loads two shells and stands over Benchley. "The two of you look away," he says.

"Wait a second," Dawes says.

"Ain't no time fore last goodbyes," Pratchet says as he cocks the shotgun.

Benchley gulps air, in little gasps, his eyes following the barrels of the shotgun hovering inches from his face.

Dawes fishes around in his cousin's collar and rips off a silver chain with a locket attached.

Benchley reaches with his good arm for the locket. He mouths words at his cousin, but no sound comes out, just pink froth at his lips.

Dawes walks away without meeting his cousin's eyes and he turns his back.

Benchley's arm falls to the earth. His eyes reflect the barrels of the shotgun.

Pratchet pulls the trigger.

. . .

Jeremiah shades his gaze against the setting sun as they ride up the creek towards town.

"What do you see, Sherif?" the deputy asks.

Jeremiah watches the shadows of the mountains sawing at the land. He looks at his deputy--what is he? Twenty-two? The kid rides like a sapling is growing up where his spine should be. Still a boy. Still got that round face and shallow eyes.

Jeremiah looks at the river, the water is low so late in the year.

"Sherif, look" the boy says, gesturing to the water.

Jeremiah looks down, expecting to see the red-backs of salmon, but no. The water is red, and there is not a fish in sight.

They round the river bend and the boy pulls up short, his face white as fresh cream. Horse corpses and the broken remains of the mail wagon dam up the stream, the water cascading over them and whipping a pink froth that clings to the rocks along the river bank. Jeremiah dismounts and hands the deputy his reins. Caltrops made from old rusted nails wound together with telegraph wire litter the road.

The corpse of a man lies on it's back, arms and legs spread like wagon spokes. His head is gone from the jaw up. Bits of skull, teeth, brain and blood littler the road. Jeremiah inspects the wound. It's sloppy work. Twelve gauge shot is imbedded in the packed earth and in the bone. The man is dressed like an Indian with beads and horsehair laced through the conchos on his belt. He's wearing moccasins with the tell-tale signs of stirrup marks on their instep. The sherif pulls the cuffs away from the man's wrists. The only thing Indian about the body was the clothes he wore. His skin was white from the wrists up.

...

Dawes, DeWitt and Pratchet cut the beads from their buckskins and moccasins before burning them. The take is almost 5,000.00$ in cash and coin. Dawes burns the letters. Pratchet hides one in his boots while Dawes is counting coins.

They pass a bottle around the fire that night.

"What are you going to do with your share of the money?" Pratchet asks DeWitt.

"Gonna buy me a farm. A nice little piece of land. Gonna get me a wife," DeWitt says. "I'm done with whores."

Pratchet snorts. "I've been married four...no five times now. Little piece of advice just between you and me, stick with the whores. You don't pay them to fuck you, you pay them leave when you're done."

Dawes laughs. He's a young man, 18, maybe 20, but a man. His eyes are hard and brown as the dry earth and his face lean with a fighter's build.

Pratchet eyes him--he'd been handsome like that once before the war, before Andersonville. Even had a sweetheart--a proper sweetheart. What was her name? All he could remember of her now was a fuzzy outline of satin skirts, auburn curls and the smell of violets. Was that her name? Violet? Viola? Vula? He shakes his head. That was another life, a life of yellow roses and the sound of cotton bowls rattling under the Carolina sun.

"Dawes," Pratchet asks. "What are you gonna do with your share?"

"Gonna get me a fine steak and one of them Celestial whores with the tiny feet and I'm gonna tickle them till' she squeals."

The men lie down that night around the dying fire.

When Dawes wakes the next morning, DeWitt's throat is slit and Pratchet is gone.

1919

Annie watched a man astride a long-legged black horse riding along the ridge. She shaded her eyes against the sun. She stepped towards him, as if to try and discern by the shadow he cast, if it was her father come back home. The man pulled his horse up short and started down the ridge. Annie dropped the pail and ran into the house. Her mother came out, wiping her calloused hands on a linen apron and she squinted into the blue desert sky. The girl tugged at her fingers and both stared at the man and black horse as he disappeared into a dip.

Mrs. Cattingale wiped her hands on her apron. It was not him, it couldn't be. She got the telegram. They sent her the telegram. She bit her lower lip. Maybe it could be. Maybe they got the wrong man. Maybe.

The rider stopped at the gate. He was thin and his shirt all soaked with sweat. He tipped his hat. Annie ran o him.

"Pa," she yelled.

The horse sidestepped. The rider looked down.

Mrs. Cattingale chased after her daughter.

"Morning," said the rider.

Mrs. Cattingale grabbed Annie's hand before she ran any closer.

"You're not my pa," said Annie. Her lower lip quivered.

"My name's Jasper, Jasper Walk," he said. "I'm looking for work."

"What kind of work?" Mrs. Cattingale asked.

He smiled. "I can turn my hand to most anything."

She looked him up and down. Too skinny. Boy that age aught to have filled out. "Times have been tough," she said.

He looked around the scrubby sagebrush, the yellow dust that covered everything and the rocky ground that couldn't even grow grass. "I'm hungry, I don't want no charity. I'll work for you iffin you got something to spare."

Mrs. Cattingale nodded. "We got beans and bacon."

Jasper pointed to the slat-rail fence, "That looks like it could use some mending."

Mrs. Cattingale nodded as she gripped her daughter's shoulder.

"Momma that hurts," said Annie.

Jasper worked the morning, ran the whole western fence line. Mrs. Cattingale brought him out a plate of beans and bacon with a biscuit. He sat in the shade of the porch and wolfed it down the way her daddy described the boys at Andersonville. The boy's horse was a leggy beast with erect ears and a smart muzzle and she counted every rib. What a shame. A damn shame.

"I told you, I told you," said Annie.

Sarah turned.

Annie dragged Regina through the doorway. Regina, all of fifteen, her coal-black waves fell around a freckled face grown cold beyond her years. She stared at the stranger as he finished his plate-- damn near licked it clean.

His eyes met those of Regina and she dropped her gaze. Her cheeks flushed red in the shade.

"I can't pay you," Sarah said. "My husband, he's-- he went to the war. We got work though, and food, plenty of both."

Jasper nodded.

"Why didn't you go?" Regina asked, stepping off the porch into the sun. The sun shown through her blue gingham dress, all washed out and patched in the shoulders with two rows of stitch-marks on the hem.

"Gina, don't ask impertinent questions."

Regina's blue eyes locked on his face. "Why didn't you go?"

Jasper tightened the girth strap on his saddle and looked up at the Monashees.

"Bet you run to Mexico with the rest of them cowards."

"I ain't no coward," he said, glaring back at her.

Regina crossed her arms.

Sarah stepped between them, "Please excuse my daughter, she's--"

Jasper mounted up. "Ain't nothing to excuse. I'm sorry for your loss."

"Why don't you stay a bit," said Sarah, "We got work. Plenty of work."

Jasper looked down at Sarah and Regina, and little Annie barely bigger than a rabbit. He nodded. Regina crinkled her nose and turned back into the house, letting the screen door slam behind her.

Sarah followed.

"You shouldn't have done that, Momma," said Regina as she scrubbed the stranger's plate. She tucked a black wave behind her ear and stared out the window as the stranger rode out to the pasture.

Sarah rubbed her temples.

Regina dunked the plate in the washing water. "If Pa was here--"

"Well he ain't, Gina."

Regina's cheeks flushed. "If he was--."

The screen door squeaked open.

"It's been a year, if he was coming home, he would have done it by now."

Annie stood in the doorway with a basket of eggs, her lower lip shaking as her eyes teared up. She dropped the basket and ran into the yard. The eggs spilled out of the straw and cracked on the floor. Some were sea green with brown speckles, the others were the color of desert clays after a rain. Regina tossed the plate into the sink and stormed out of the kitchen.

. . .

Jabber set to work on the pasture fence line. He breathed the free air as blue skies stretched beyond and white clouds dotted the horizon like mice in a hayloft. He saw someone running across the farmyard, someone small. She slipped through a gap in the fence and ran halfway across the pasture at full gallop to a craggy apple tree. She climbed into the low branches and set there. Jabber kept working the slat. He planed down the end with a hatchet and shaved off the chips with his knife and moved on to the next one. She was still in the tree, her arms wrapped around her tan little legs. She wore no shoes. The door slammed on the farmhouse and Regina stormed towards the barn. Annie climbed further up the tree and hid in the leaves. Jabber looked at the next slat-rail lying loose in it's socket, turned around. He road to the apple tree.

Annie looked down at him.

Jabber dismounted and smiled.

"What's his name?" she asked.

"He don't have one." Jabber, pet the long neck of the prairie mustang. "You mind keeping him company for a bit?"

Annie shook her head.

Jabber removed the bridal. "He like's apples."

Jabber walked the fence line of foot under the dry heat but not a bead of sweat broke out on his back. He looked over his shoulder; the mustang grazed in the shade of the apple tree as apples fell from the rustling branches above.

Sarah rang a triangle for supper just as the light faded. Jabber turned back for the apple tree. The eastern edge of the sky was purple and the first stars peaked out like pearls. Jabber stopped under the tree.

Annie held out her hands to him and he lifted her down--she weighed nothing. He set her on the saddle and lead her back to the house. She pet the mustang's neck.

"You should give him a name," she said. "He's a good horse."

"I ain't no good with names. Why don't you give him one," said Jabber.

She stroked the dark main, let the hair flow through her fingers and it shined.

"How about Fred?" Annie asked.

Jabber counted back over the men he'd known with that name. "It's a good name."

Jabber lifted her off the saddle and placed her on the ground again--she was such a tiny thing. Annie hugged the mustang's neck. The horse snorted and nuzzled her ear. Jabber lead him away into the barn.

Sarah waited in the doorway. "You'll sleep in here," she said, gesturing to the tack-room. A small bed built from wood slats and four feed barrels set in one corner. A bar of gritty soap lay next to a wash basin and ewer on a sun-beleached cabinet. "Sorry it ain't much," she said.

"Ma'am, it's better than I've had in a long time."

"I'll let you get washed up before dinner," she said as she left. She stopped in the doorway and said over her shoulder, her brows furrowed, "Don't pay any mind to what Regina says."

The family sat around the dinner table as Jabber entered the house.

Regina looked him up and down, "You took your sweet time."

Annie glared at her across the table.

"Mind your manners, Gina," Sarah said. "Everybody hold hands and say grace."

Regina bowed her head. Annie clutched Jabber's hand and held it firm. Sarah took his other hand and bowed her head.

"Dear Lord," Sarah started, "Bless this meal we are about to eat--."

"And look after Pa," Annie said.

Sarah shifted in her seat, "And please keep in Your grace, oh Lord, the soul Frederik Cattingale. Amen."

Regina pressed her lips together until they were white. Sarah passed the potatoes and buttered greens around the table. Regina handed them on, her plate empty.

"Gina, honey, aren't you going to eat?"

Regina stared across the table at Jabber, "I'm not hungry."

Sarah straightened up in her chair and looked her daughter in the eyes, "Then you are excused."

. . .

Jabber tucked his pistols under the pillow and stuffed his knife between the mattress and the board. The lamp light burned beside his bed as he hovered on the edge of sleep. Darkness flickered in the corners, creeping around the edges of the circle of light where shadows raced across the baseboards, coalescing in one corner of the room. She rose from the darkness with hungry, grasping arms, her chestnut hair plaited like like hemp-rope and draped over her shoulder. Her dress fluttered around her bare legs all in tatters and her lips moved without sound.

"Forgive me," he said. "Bessie, forgive me."

. . .

A stranger approached the Pratchet house with a saddle slung over his shoulder.

When he knocked, Old Man Pratchet answered.

"Sorry to trouble you sir, but my horse--she broke a leg," the stranger said and he smiled.

Old Man Pratchet looked him over. "You live round here?"

"Just passing through," the stranger said. He reached out a hand, "My name's Bobby Lee."

Old Man Pratchet didn't shake his hand. "Where you from Mr. Bobby Lee?"

Bobby Lee retracted his hand and said, "Kelowna."

Silence passed between them as Old Man Pratchet eyed him--there was something about the boy he didn't like, he just couldn't put his finger on what.

A coyote howled in the night. Another answered in the dark.

Bobby Lee looked over his shoulder, "Guessin' they found my horse." He sighed, his shoulders bowed under the weight of the saddle and hours walking in those boots. "Please sir," he said and the weariness crept into his voice like the prairie dust that covered everything in the end. "I've been walking for hours, this here farm is the first lights I've seen. I won't be no trouble, honest. I just need a place to lay my head for the night. I got money."

The lines around Old Man Pratchet's eyes softened as he peered at the stranger.

"How much."

"I'll give you three dollars if you'll spare me a biscuit or some corn bread and let me sleep in the barn."

"Make it five dollars and you got yourself a deal," the old man replied.

"Ain't got five dollars," said Bobby Lee.

"Guess you're shit out of luck then, ain't you son," the old man said as he shut the door.

"Wait," said Bobby Lee. He reached into his shirt with a grimy hand and pulled out a tarnished chain. Swinging from it like a cherry pit was a small silver locket. "Make a trade?" he asked.

The old man's eyes flashed off the silver. "We can make a trade," he said gesturing for the boy to hand it over.

Bobby Lee smiled and pulled the chain over his head. The locket swung in the darkness between them, back and forth like a pendulum.

The old man reached for it.

Bobby let go of the chain.

The locket fell into the dust at the old man's feet.

Old Man Pratchet swore as he knelt to fetch it from the dust. It was a foolish thing…careless. The butt of a pistol slammed down on the back of his head and the last thing he remembered was the taste of dust.

Old Man Pratchet came to on the dirt floor of his own damn house. His mouth tasted of blood and dirt and the trill in his ears whined like a choir of mosquitos. He sat up.

Bobby Lee sat at his table smoking a pipe. "Where is the money, old man."

Pratchet looked at the door where a weather beaten saddle rested against the packed earth. "Ain't got no money." The old man said.

"Bullshit you ain't," Bobby Lee replied.

Pratchet squinted at him, the light from the oil lamp stung his eyes. "I told you there ain't no money!" Pratchet yelled.

Bobby Lee stood, his shadow covered half the room. "Tell me where the money is or I start cutting off toes." Bobby Lee pulled a knife. The blade glinted fresh from the whetstone.

Pratchet shook his head. Men like that didn't waste the bullets. He knew. Lord he knew. "I spent it all," he said, "been gone for years."

Bobby Lee's shadow trembled like it was laughing, but it wasn't laughter that came out of that mouth. "What the fuck did you spend five-thousand dollars on?" Bobby asked.

Pratchet laughed and slapped the earth with his leathery hand, "Five-thousand? Boy who told you that? It was five hundred and I spent it. It's gone."

Bobby Lee's shadow bounced and writhed in the lamp light, but his hand when it drew that blade back was steady as a rail.

"You shouldn't lie to the boy, Tom," a voice said from the shadows. A man all dressed in black lifted the glass from the oil lamp and lit a cigarillo. The scent of cinnamon and cloves mixed with the odor of tobacco as it wafted around the room. "He don't like liars."

"Dawes," said the old man. "Thought they hanged you."

Dawes pulled the bandanna down from his throat, revealing a shining red scar.

Old Man Pratchet grunted.

"Where's the money," Dawes asked. "No lies this time."

"It's gone," Old Man Pratchet said. Sweat poured down his face, working its way into the wrinkles and itching.

Coyotes howled in the distance.

Dawes puffed away on that cigarillo, the orange tip of it burned like a live coal from the devil's furnace.

"As God's my witness," Pratchet said.

"Don't you be swearing to God now, Tom," Dawes said as he stubbed out the rest of his cigarillo. "He don't like liars either."

...

Jabber road out at dawn as the farmyard slept. Clouds swathed the Monashees to the north. The sun rose in the east and the clouds darkened, coiling around jagged peaks, never moving on. Jabber tended his work with his back to the north. He looked over his shoulder now and again, and the roiling thunderheads wound ever tighter around one peak in particular--he didn't have to guess which one--and the longer he watched them, the less they looked like clouds.

Jabber turned his back on the clouds and the mountains, but they would always be there waiting for him.

. . .

Sarah rang the triangle for supper just as the first flashes of lighting struck the valley.

The women gathered at the table, Annie helped set. She folded Jasper's napkin into a little star.

"Stop it," said Regina as she unfolded the napkin and laid it flat next to his plate.

Annie frowned and snatched the napkin back again.

Regina tore it away from her.

"Regina Cattingale," Sarah said, leveling a wooden spoon at her daughter from the kitchen, "Get in here and see to the chicken."

Annie folded the napkin into a star and laid it next to Jasper's plate.

The women folk sat down at the table as the thunder rolled in the distance. They waited.

Jasper's chair sat empty.

Annie stared out the kitchen window.

No light shone from the barn.

"Maybe he's gone to bed," said Sarah.

Regina shook her head.

"Regina, why don't you bring him a plate?" Sarah asked.

Annie jumped up. "I'll do it." She knocked over her chair and grabbed his plate.

Sarah looked to Regina. "Go with her."

"Momma--."

"I said go."

Regina carried the lantern and the plate.

"I can do it," said Annie as she trailed behind her.

Regina held her head high, "You'll spill it everywhere."

Annie pouted. "I wouldn't."

The tack room door stood ajar. Annie stepped inside. "Jasper?"

The bed sat empty.

Annie's face bleached white. She ran passed her sister and into the barn.

Regina set the plate beside the wash basin. Maybe he'd cleared out. Good.

Annie ran back to the door. "Fred's still here."

Thunder clapped outside, loud, just over the ridge above. The flash illuminated the barn.

"If he is around, he'll find his damn dinner," Regina said, grabbing Annie's arm.

They left the tack room door ajar as they departed.

Jabber watched them go, both guns cocked and clenched in white knuckles from the shadows under the bed.

. . .

Sarah sat before the fireplace as the thunder clapped in the distance. The storm moved on without a drop of rain. The girls slept. Sarah pulled down the box from the mantle, the one he gave her on their wedding day. She removed his service photo and the letters. She read every one. The thunder died away in the distance. The flashes dimmed. She finished the last letter and lifted the telegram. Three sentences in teletype. She'd read them a hundred times, a thousand. She read them again and removed her wedding ring and placed it in the bottom of the box next to his service photograph. A raw white line shone on her finger in the lamp light, blushing red and accusing at the edges. Twenty years--twenty--gone. She laid the letters on top of the picture, the telegram and the ring and shut the box.

. . .

Annie and Regina sat at the breakfast table as Jabber entered. Regina bent over a piece of yellowing paper with a pencil in hand.

"We missed you at supper last night," Sarah said.

Jabber nodded. "Sorry about that."

She handed him a plate with a warm biscuit and she smiled. "Coffee's on the table."

Jabber ate his breakfast as Annie copied letters out of the bible on an old envelope. She wrote her S's backwards.

Sarah washed up at the sink.

"We're going into town tomorrow for Sunday service," said Sarah.

"I still got work to do," Jabber said.

Regina muttered under her breath.

"Finished," said Annie.

Sarah turned from the kitchen. "Gina, can you read it?"

The black curtain of Regina's hair fell over her left shoulder. "I'm busy."

"I'll read it," said Jabber.

Regina snorted.

Annie handed it to him. All the letters mashed together into one long word, slanting across the envelope.

Jabber drew a line across the back of the envelope. "Lets write your name," he said.

Annie smiled and sat up in her seat. Jabber stood behind her, holding the pencil, and guided her hand just the way Bessie used to do for him.

With patient strokes, he guided Annie's little hand, first the A, then the N's. Regina watched them.

"Momma, momma I wrote my name," said Annie. She stood up on her chair and hugged Jabber around the neck and ran into the kitchen to show Sarah the envelope.

Jabber stood there blushing, his hands resting on the back of the chair. His work hand trembled.

Regina stared at him.

Jabber opened his mouth like he was going to say something, and felt the stutter coming on. He downed his coffee in one go and marched out to the barn.

Jabber tipped a pint of oats into the plough horse's trough as he passed. It was a large animal, part quarter horse, part morgan by the look of it, with a gray coat and brown spots--not a particularly smart creature, but it had a softness that only came to animals treated kindly by the world. Jabber patted it's neck and checked it's forelegs. Light filtered through the barn doorway, yellow and soft as corn silk.

The horse snorted as Jabber checked its hooves. Jabber looked up.

Regina was a shadow wreathed in golden light. She held a basket under he left arm. "Mamma says to get your washing."

Jabber nodded.

She vanished into the tack room.

Jabber lifted a dozen fence posts into the back of the wagon. When he looked up again, Regina was standing there.

"Your clothes to," she said.

"I'll see to them," Jabber replied.

"You ain't seen to them in a while," she said.

"That's my business," said Jabber as he lead the plough horse out into the farm yard.

Annie fed the chickens in the shade of the kitchen garden. They pecked around her bare feet. She waved to him.

Sarah hung the first batch of linens out to dry on lines strung from the south west corner of the house. The wind blew out of the north and no clouds curled around the Monashees. Jabber set about his chores.

Sarah was waiting for him when he came in for the night.

"If you live under our roof, Jasper Walk, you go to church."

Jabber lead the plough horse back to the stall and un-harnessed him without meeting her eyes. "I ain't the church going sort."

Her face hardened. "You're coming to church tomorrow and the next time Regina asks for your washing, you let her see to it."

When Jabber washed up for dinner, the bed was made up with fresh linens and set on the edge, folded like store-bought, a plaid shirt and pair of trousers patched at the left knee. Jabber lifted them up. They were too big around the waist for him, but they'd fit and they smelled like soap. Jabber smiled.

When the triangle rang for breakfast the next morning, Jabber walked in washed. He'd combed his hair and cleaned under his nails and he smelled like soap instead of horse. Regina looked up at him as he entered and dropped her eyes, blushing.

Jabber sat at the table without a word. The girls wore their best dresses. Annie wore a pink cap-sleeved dress with a pink ribbon around her middle and her hair was all done up in braids. Bessie wore a blue dress, the color of lupine in the spring. She'd braided her black hair and pinned it along the top of her head like a crown. Sarah's dress was brown and modest. Bright colors were for the young.

Jabber brought the wagon out after breakfast. Sarah took the reins. Jabber rode along side.

"Mamma, can I ride with Jasper?" Annie asked.

"No, honey, you'll muss your dress."

The sky opened bright blue forever and the air smelled of sage and wild flowers. Jabber breathed deep. They headed down a dusty road along a creek where the sage brush swept away through tall brown grass, still green along the creek. Scrubby sumac and kinniknnick grew between lodgepole pine and wild cherry as they passed abandoned homesteads with black tar boards and sway-backed roofs. Jabber turned up the creek.

Sarah called. "Where you goin?" Jabber glanced up Ruby road. Fireweed grew tall and pink up the center and the old wagon ruts were channel scars. Jabber stared up that road as the women trundled past in the trap, he stared at the abandoned cabins, the flat spots where white tents once stood. The air still smelled the same. The trees still grew tall. Everything else had changed.

The mustang pawed the earth and threw it's head. Jabber turned his horse and joined the women on the river road.

Sarah looked at him from under her bonnet. "Jasper, how old are you?"

He spurred the mustang ahead and kept his own council.

...

They reached Kumaq before noon. Jabber rode up the streets ahead of the wagon. Red brick buildings replaced the old wooden storefronts. On the spot of the Silver Dollar saloon stood a new school house. The dance hall was converted to a church and gone were the trade tipi's along the river. The stock yard still stood, so did the grange and as he rode past the courthouse and jail, that black oak stood a little taller and straighter, but time couldn't erase the rope burns on it's branches. Folks couldn't white-wash the town and call it respectable, not when the cemetery was filled with men who died the hard way digging for gold in El Dorado.

On the outskirts of town, the white revival tent billowed like rising bread. Hundreds gathered, the men in their white button-down shirts and black slacks, their wives in long dresses with their hair done up and the daughters in every shade of summer and springtime. Jabber hitched the mustang to a post. He lifted Annie out of the wagon and set her on the ground. She walked over to the mustang and pet his neck.

"You won't be lonely out here, will you Fred?"

The mustang snorted and nuzzled her ear. She pet his cheek and laughed.

Jabber reached for Regina's hand.

"I can do it myself, thanks," she said without looking at him.

Jabber stepped aside.

Sarah took his hand when he offered it.

The eyes of several parishioners watched them as they entered the tent, Sarah leading the way and Annie holding Jabber's hand. Whispers fluttered as they sat down together.

Regina's cheeks blushed beneath her bonnet.

The preacher stood before the congregation in his short sleeves, and collar. He raised the bible and laid it down on the podium. He lifted his hands to high heaven and let loose a sermon full of fire and the wrath of God.

Jabber crossed his arms and stared that minister down and when everyone else was saying their amens, Jabber's lips never parted.

Services ended with folks getting saved. Three women fainted when he laid hands on them. They followed that preacher down to the river and he dunked them in the cold waters with their arms crossed upon their chests. Jabber stood on the banks above, and the preacher never once strayed into his shadow.

The women gossiped for a spell in pioneer park eating potato salad and drinking cider. Jabber set in the shade and pulled an old worn bible out of his saddle bags. Annie sat with him.

"Momma says I can start school," Annie said. "Did you ever go to school?"

Jabber thumbed a page. "Nope."

She frowned. "I'll ask Momma, maybe you can come too."

Jabber shook his head.

Regina moved through the line at the long tables, her long dark hair a rainbow of cinnamon, chocolate and coffee. Two men stood in line behind her. The skin of their faces was tanned from long days in the sun and their hands were large and weather-beaten, but it was the way their hats were pulled over their brows and those twitchy fingers that made Jabber sit up and take notice. One of them leaned in close and whispered something to Regina. She looked up at him and turned her back. Jabber smiled--proud girl. Annie waved to Regina, but Regina sat by herself under one of the old oak trees along the white gravel path. The two men followed. Jabber's hand grazed his belt for phantom guns. "Go on and find your momma," he said to Annie as he rose.

A shadow strayed into the sun and stood over them. Jabber looked up. It was a man's shape.

Jabber's back tightened. "Can I help you?"

"What's your name son?" the man asked. Jabber shaded his eyes. The man was older, with hard lines etched into the corners of his weathered face. His hair might have been blond once, but it was white now, save for a few graying wisps along his ears.

"Who's asking?"

The man's hands rested on narrow hips and the trigger finger of his right hand tapped his leather belt with a familiar sound.

Jabber's work-hand twitched.

"Morning, Jeremiah," said Sarah as she approached, holding a plate of potato salad.

The sheriff tipped his hat, "Sarah."

She smiled.

"Jeremiah, this is Jasper Walk. Jasper, this is Sheriff Ward."

Jabber stood up. They were of a height and out of the sheriff's shadow, Jabber saw his face and there was something familiar about it.

The sheriff extended a hand.

Jabber looked the sheriff in the eye as they shook and felt the smooth patch on the first knuckle crease of his trigger finger.

"You got kin around this parts, Mr. Walk?" Sheriff Ward asked.

Jabber shook his head.

"What brings you to Kumaq?"

"Work," said Jabber.

"Work," the sheriff repeated, eyes on Jasper and his trigger finger tapping his belt.

Annie looked from the sheriff to Jabber and back again to the sheriff. She grasped Jabber's work-hand and squeezed it.

"Something the matter, sheriff?" Sarah asked.

"Been some trouble up by Loomis," he said. "Strange folk about."

Sarah nodded. "Pratchet. I heard. God rest his soul."

The sheriff looked Jasper over one more time. "Ya'll have a good one."

Sarah handed Jabber the plate of potato salad. "What was that about?"

Jabber stood up and handed Annie to her mother.

"Where you going?" Annie asked.

"Just going to talk to Regina," Jabber said, marching across the grass.

One of the men leaned against the tree, the other stood in front of her. She looked down at her plate and picked at her potato salad without eating it.

"Regina," Jabber said, "Your momma asked me to fetch you."

The two men turned with a start. Jabber stood with the sun at his back. They shielded their eyes and their hands went right to their hips.

"You mind, friend, we're talking to the lady," said the one leaning against the tree.

"Regina?" Jabber asked, his hand outstretched.

She stood and walked to Jabber without a word.

"You interrupted a private conversation," said the man leaning against the tree. He kept a dark mustache and darker eyes. He might have been forty--too old to be talking up a seventeen-year old girl. The other was younger, maybe twenty-five, with a liar's face. He smiled too easy and too quick.

"Go on," Jabber said, "your momma's waiting. I'll be over in a minute."

Regina nodded, glancing over her shoulder as she walked away.

"Mighty rude of you, stranger," said the one with the dark mustache as he leaned against the tree. He kept a black kerchief wound around his neck.

Jasper looked into those dark eyes and said, "Move on. Your intentions ain't welcome."

The liar's face contorted about the edges and his shadow seemed to dance on the cool grass. His companion placed a hand on his shoulder as the young man reached into his coat pocket.

"Our sincerest apologies," said the older man. "Didn't mean to cause the lady no discomfort, honest." He pulled his companion to the side and the two of them walked off behind the old court house in the shadow of the hanging tree.

Jabber turned back to the picnic in pioneer park, and standing there with a plate of potato salad, watching him like an old barn cat was Sherif Ward.

...

The family rode the eighteen miles home in silence, Jasper leading the wagon by three lengths, eyes ever on the north as the horse, ears erect, gnashed at the bit. Man and beast loped along one creature yoked together by time and torment. Regina sat beside her mother, blue eyes staring at the clouds.

"Looks like it's gonna storm," Regina said.

"Bad one by the looks of it," said Sarah.

The first rumble of thunder broke and Jasper kicked that mustang into a gallop.

When Sarah rang the triangle for supper, Jasper did not appear. Annie set a place for him special. He didn't come. The storm rolled down the valley, iron gray thunderheads and fork lightning but never a drop of rain.

"Where is that man?" Sarah asked.

"I'll go fetch him," Annie said.

Regina rose from the table.

"I can do it myself," Annie said. Her little lips pulling down into a pout.

"I know you can," said Regina. She carried her empty plate in to the kitchen and put it away in the cupboard.

"Regina, hun, ain't you hungry?" Sarah asked.

Regina shook her head.

Annie ran out the screen door. It slammed behind her as thunder rumbled three ridges over. Unnatural dark blanketed the land and at the edges, the last red rays of sun poured through like a forge and in those clouds faces roiled.

Annie burst through the tack-room door, "Jasper," she called.

A lamp burned by the wash basin. His saddle set on a saw horse by the wall. Jasper was no where to be seen.

Annie sat down on the floor and pouted, her tan little arms wrapped around her legs. The light flickered as the wind whispered through the boards and set the shadows to dancing along the walls. Something flashed beneath the bed. Annie glanced at it. Jasper lay there in the dark, pistols drawn, staring at the underside of the saw-boards.

"What are you doing under there?" she asked.

Jasper didn't reply.

"You afraid of the storm?" she asked.

He nodded.

Annie frowned and crawled on her hands and knees under the bed beside him. Jasper stiffened as she hugged him. She lay her cornsilk hair against his shoulder and draped a slender arm across his chest. "You don't have to be afraid," she said. "I'll stay with you." She smiled.

"You should go back to the house," Jasper said, holstering his guns and tucking the hosters as far away from her as his arms would allow.

She gripped his shirt in her small fist, the soft flannel bunched up in her fingers. She nestled her forehead into his shoulder and closed her eyes. She thought about her father. Tried to remember him, but all she saw was Jasper's face smiling down at her in the sun from that army uniform.

"Jasper?" a woman called.

The boards creaked. Scuffed brown boots appeared in the doorway beneath the hem of a blue gingham dress.

"Bessie?" Jasper asked.

"Who's Bessie?" Annie asked.

The woman in the blue gingham dress dropped to her knees. Sable hair fell around her face and brushed the floor. "What are you two doing under there?" Regina asked.

"Jasper doesn't like storms," Annie said.

Regina smiled, and there was a softness in her face. "Come on, it's supper time." She reached for Annie.

Annie grabbed another fist full of Jasper's shirt. "I'm staying."

"Come on, Momma made a nice supper. You can't eat it under the bed."

"I said I'm staying."

"Jasper," Regina said. "Will you get out from under that bed, please?"

Jasper exhaled and nodded. He lifted Annie up with one arm as he eased across the floorboards. He handed her to Regina, and climbed out from under that bed.

"Grown man like you afraid of storms?" Regina asked with a smile.

"I ain't a coward if that's what you're implying," Jasper said.

The smile vanished from her face, and she dropped her eyes. "I wasn't."

Annie grabbed Jabber's hand. Her fingers tightened around his trigger finger and she tugged him towards the door. "Come on," she said.

Jasper flinched as a flash of lightning sent the shadows crawling for the corners.

Regina grabbed Annie's other hand. "If he doesn't want his dinner, that's his business."

Annie frowned. "Jasper Walk, you come to dinner. You come to dinner right now!"

He looked down at her and then out into the darkened barn. He scooped her up into his arms and carried her towards the house.

...

Sarah sat on the back porch with a wooden spoon in one hand. If that boy didn't come in for dinner...

Lightning flashed and they were there, soundless and staring, as if risen from shadows and clay. Their eyes burned with some intent and purpose Sarah would never question or hope to call on. Three men on dark horses set before her, and these men--if men they were--wore long oil cloth dusters and the wide brimmed hats so favored by her grandfather and his kin…God rest their souls. Each man had a face hard as saddle leather, creased and folded at the corners from long years of riding beyond pain, beyond thirst and weariness. She'd seen such faces before, on men of God or men of law.

"What can I do for you gentlemen?" she asked.

They stared at her with coal-fire eyes.

"We've come for Jasper Walk," said the man with the long mustache, he was older than the rest and his voice rasped and boomed like the fading echo of a thunder clap.

Jasper appeared in the barn doorway, carrying Annie with Regina beside him. The riders from the storm turned their gaze upon him. Lightning flashed in the din and their eyes drank up the night.

Jasper stopped. He handed Annie to Regina. "Go to your momma," he said. "They won't hurt you"

Annie grabbed a fistful of his shirt.

Jasper pulled away.

"Jasper Walk," said the old rider. His voice carried far in the stillness. The other's turned, their finger's resting on the pommels, guns at each hip and rifles at the knee. Jabber's work hand reached for his gun, but it was gone--tucked in his belt under the bed. He looked down at Annie and Regina. "You have to let me go," he said.

Annie pressed her lips together and shook her head. She tightened her fist in his shirt.

"Regina, you bring her here," Sarah called. Her voice trembled with the wind.

Regina grasped Jasper's right hand and she stepped in front of him. "You can't have him," she said to the rider.

Annie wrapped both arms around Jasper's leg and held fast.

The rider's set there on their dark horses, their dusters ruffling with the wind.

"Regina," Sarah yelled. "You get over here right now or so help me God."

Thunder cracked in the distance; red fire bloomed from the mountain and Regina stayed at Jasper's side.

Sarah marched right off that porch straight to her daughters. She grabbed Regina by the hand. "Regina Cattingale, you let go of that man."

Regina looked her dead in the eyes, "No."

Sarah smacked her across the face.

Regina's cheek burned red as she twisted her hand out of her mother's grasp and grabbed hold of Jasper's arm.

Sarah glared down at her youngest child, pretzeled around Jasper's right leg. She looked at Regina--proud Regina--with the bruise already spreading across her cheek.

"Jasper Walk," she said, "You step away from my girls."

"Don't let them take him, Momma," Annie yelled.

Sarah looked from Jasper to the riders and back again to Jasper. Whatever he was, he wasn't a coward.

Sarah turned her back on Jasper and her children and with her hands on her hips, she said to those riders, "Ya'll are trespassing on my land. Clear off."

Silent as they'd come, one by one they turned into the storm and as the darkness settled about them beyond the light of the kitchen window, their oil cloth dusters and their dark horses fleshed with the sky until they were all but invisible in the naked night.

...

Sarah didn't say a word when she came for the buggy at dawn. She hitched the old plough horse up herself and didn't look back once as she trotted down the road towards town. Jabber packed his things in the tack room. He left the pants and shirt they'd lent him on the bed. He took a broom to the corners and swept under the bed. He wiped the soot from the kerosene lamp and folded the blankets up neat. When he was done, he surveyed his work. It was still early, he might make Omak before night-fall. Not a cloud broke the eastern sky, but that didn't mean much. The smell of storm still lingered on the air, and his horse pawed the earth. He holstered his guns, donned his hat and stepped out into the cool morning.

"Thought you said you weren't no coward?" Regina said as she brought out the chicken slops.

"They'll be back," Jabber said. He tightened the girth strap on his saddle and ran his hand over the mustang's foreleg.

"Momma went for the sheriff," Regina said.

"All the better I leave now then."

"I don't know what you done, Jasper Walk, but you done right by us."

He turned his back as he climbed in the saddle.

Her blue eyes widened and the light bounced off them, blue as desert morning.

She bit her lower lip. "If I--if I asked you to stay…"

He looked down at her--even with that bruise across her face, she was beautiful. He tipped his hat. "Take care of your sister." Jabber headed for the road and cut south. He turned back once and saw Regina standing with the bucket, her shoulders shaking.

. . .

Dawes took up position by the door after Annie carried the egg basket out the back door. As soon as she laid eyes on the Boby Lee, Annie yelped and ran for the house screaming, "Regina! Regina!" and there was Dawes ready to snatch her up.

Regina ran out of the house holding a kitchen knife.

"Ain't no need for that, young lady," Dawes said. "Now put it down."

She spun on her heel, her eyes murderous.

Dawes cocked his pistol and held it to the girl's head. "Drop. The. Knife."

Annie cried, squirming in his arms. Dawes tightened his grip. Annie gagged, her face turning red.

"All right. All right, stop it!" Regina said, lowering the knife and placing it on the ground. "Just give me my sister back."

"Bobby," Dawes called. "Get up here."

Bobby Lee appeared around the corner with rope in hand. He tied Regina's wrists together and handed the rope to Dawes.

Dawes lashed it to Bobby's saddle horn. "You keep an eye on that little one," he said.

"She squirms like damned fish," said Bobby Lee. "Now you listen to me girl!" he yelled at Annie as he shook her, "You stop that, you hear?"

Annie kicked and bit him. Bobby Lee smacked her and she fell to the earth.

Regina screamed.

Jabber wasn't two miles away when he heard a woman's shriek echoing along the boulders. He turned that horse around and spurred it to a gallop back towards the farm.

Bobby Lee made to backhand Regina but Dawes stopped him.

"Don't damage the goods," said Dawes.

"How we gonna keep that whore quiet?" he asked.

Dawes sighed and pulled the kerchief from his neck, revealing the shining band where stubble no longer grew. He gagged Regina and he and Bobby Lee tied Annie's wrists and ankles together and they slung her over the back of Bobby Lee's saddle.

They took the girl's north.

Jabber reached the farm house in double quick time, but the girls were gone. Blood stained the ground by the kitchen door and the crumpled shape of a girl was printed in the dust. Jabber thumbed the hammer on his pistols. He mounted up and followed Regina's footprints in the dust.

When the road split up Smoke Canyon, Dawes headed off towards the Similkameen. "You keep on going," he said.

Bobby Lee nodded and took the girls up the Smoke Road.

Regina looked over the edge of the thin band of trail as they climbed out of the canyon. The trail was littered with shale. She could jump off the edge and pull with all her weight, it might just be enough to yank horse and rider over the edge, but then there was Annie. Little Annie…she couldn't do that to her. So long as they were alive, they could get out of this. So long as they were alive, they could get back home to Mamma.

Dawes watched and he waited. He heard the rider before he saw him. He leaned into the earth with the rifle to his shoulder and he waited. Jabberwok followed the trail Bobby Lee left. He slowed his pace up that narrow track, switching back across the sheer face of the canyon wall. Dawes smiled, and he waited. Jabberwok was two switchbacks away from the top, then one. Dawes aimed. He breathed. He fired. The horse stumbled forward, shot in the chest.

Rider and horse fell together and broke upon the canyon floor.

Dawes left his perch. He holstered the rifle, whistled a short tune to himself and lead his horse down to the Smoke Road.

Jabber was still breathing when Dawes reached him, but his body was mangled with the horse.

"Don't you look the fool," Dawes said, smiling. The sun glinted off the scar on his neck. Above his head, black forms already circled. "I could put you out of your misery," he said, drawing his pistol and pointing it at Jabber's face. "Would kinda spoil the fun for them though, wouldn't it?" He nodded towards the circling birds.

Jabber coughed and blood splattered Dawes' boots.

"Sorry about your sweetheart," Dawes said, wiping his boots on Jabber's shirt. He holstered his pistol, mounted up to catch Bobby Lee. He left Jabber in the bottom of the canyon with the flies already crawling across his lips.

Jabber lay as the thunder rumbled in the distance and the skies turned green. The three ravens--if ravens they were--lit down on the rocks and then came the sound of hoof beats on the gravel. Jabber stared up into the worn faces beneath those black brimmed hats. He knew two of them, but not the third--not the old man who lead them. The old man leaned over his saddle and said, "Rise." The wind picked up out of the north, cold and cruel and smelling of wet stone and iron. The three riders waited. Jabber rose from the earth. The mustang, still bloodied threw it's head and pawed the earth where its blood already blackened the rocks. Jabber mounted up and wordlessly they lead him up the narrow ridge spur. The storm descended.

The clouds roiled green and oily and from them the herd burst like prairie fire raging across the leaden skies. Haggard men on ragged horses chased after them with parched lips and torn shirts, and Jabber fell in line behind Krickt and it was as if he'd never left them The bounty men disappeared into the dust and fading daylight.

As the herd and those who chased it rose into the sky, Jabber gazed down upon the world he had lately known before he forgot it and himself. He spied two riders, one trailing a girl on a rope, the other with a child lashed to his saddle, and he remembered. Jabberwok turned west for the old ridge-line and spurred that prairie mustang straight and true. His brothers laughed and jeered him onward--them that had ridden since forever and a day--and up that draw he scrambled until they met under the last cruel rays of desert sun and onward under the rising horns of the moon. In his heart--for he still had one--he remembered her blue eyes. He remembered her coal black hair falling around her ruddy face and how when she looked at him, he meant something…and he meant to do something now.

That's the night that the lights went out across the Basin. That's the night Jabberwok caught the Devil's Herd. He ran that mustang across the stony outcrops and steel hooves kicked up flints that sparked alight across a clear evening sky. He pushed that horse straight on to burning and the very flesh crisped and fell from his bones...but they rode beyond pain and patience--single minded, by heaven-come-hell--to catch the forsaken herd. He drew upon them with a whip like wings of fire and cracked a'thunder from ridge to ridge and shook the rocks and trees and windows as he passed, racing along that fell-divide between the waking world and the hereafter where foul dreams and accursed beeves sought a moment's refuge in the fading light. And now he drove them onward across those endless skies. They groaned and snorted sparks and steam and rolled those reddened eyes where all the torments of hell reflected the hateful jewels of men's deceit and guile. Jabberwok reeled them south in a flourish of heat lightning as they touched down atop Mt. Chapacaw. He drove them on now, alone, as his brothers hollered for him to wait, but no, he had purpose in death he'd never had in life and she had the bluest eyes. He jumped the ridge with them thundering down towards the river like an avalanche of cloven hooves and steel and those below looked up in fear to the stars for there was fire on the mountain and lightning in the air, dead-men screaming across the valley and no respite for the wicked anywhere. Old Jabberwok he pushed them ever harder till the beeves touched the old Smoke Road and stampeded Bobby Lee Orsen and Louis Dawes into nothing but a pile of ashes, dust and bone.

And he tarried for but a moment as them beeves thundered on into the night, and his eyes met those of Regina who once had loved him…but all she saw was a damned old'ghost; burned bones and an ashen horse standing in the last red rays of fading light. He turned, and those empty-socket eyes they burned with the fires of regret, but also a little pride--that's what got him in this mess to begin with--and with a yip and a holler from that lipless jaw he rode away on the night-wind where sparks still lingered from the passing of the Devil's Herd and the Ghost Riders in the Sky.

The End

About the Author:

D. F. Bissonnette grew up in the Pacific Northwest and attended the University of Washington and holds a B.A. in Anthropology and a certificate in Popular Fiction. D.F. currently lives in Everett, Washington and enjoys hiking in the Olympic and Cascade Mountains and visiting ghost towns in Washington and Oregon.

Printed in Great Britain
by Amazon